"We've been robbed!" shouted Sabrina.

Aunt Zelda rushed over to her laptop computer, which sat in its usual spot on the kitchen table. Aunt Hilda ran to inspect the silverware, which was all clean and neatly stacked, not in its usual mixed-up jumble in the drawer.

"What's b̶_____

"The m̶_____ ealizing how silly that _____, exactly, but we have _____body came in and left these flow_____ also cleaned the kitchen and did my homework."

Aunt Hilda waved a shiny fork in the air. "This silver hasn't been polished this well in centuries. I think we have a hobby."

"What's that?" asked Sabrina.

"A hobgoblin is a household spirit who protects the home and does useful chores in the middle of the night," explained Zelda.

Sabrina tossed her blond hair. "You mean this hobgoblin is going to come in every night and clean the house, do my homework, wash the dishes, and do whatever else has to be done? You go, Hobgoblin!"

Sabrina, the Teenage Witch™ books

Available from ARCHWAY Paperbacks

Sabrina The Teenage Witch®

Haunts in
the House

John Vornholt

Based on Characters Appearing in Archie Comics

**And based upon the television series
Sabrina, The Teenage Witch
Created for television by Nell Scovell
Developed for television by Jonathan Schmock**

AN ARCHWAY PAPERBACK
Published by POCKET BOOKS
New York   London   Toronto   Sydney   Tokyo   Singapore

AN ARCHWAY PAPERBACK *Original*

An Archway Paperback published by
POCKET BOOKS, a division of Simon & Schuster Inc.
1230 Avenue of the Americas, New York, NY 10020

ISBN: 0-671-02819-7

First Archway Paperback printing October 1999

10 9 8 7 6 5 4 3 2 1

AN ARCHWAY PAPERBACK and colophon are
registered trademarks of Simon & Schuster Inc.

SABRINA THE TEENAGE WITCH and all related titles, logos
and characters are trademarks of Archie Comics Publications, Inc.

Printed in the U.S.A.

IL 4+

For Danielle

Chapter 1

When the shriek of the alarm clock blasted into her senses, Sabrina bolted upright in bed. She gazed out her bedroom window and blinked, thinking that it was way too dark for her wake up. Even the crickets were still asleep. Then why was her alarm clock ringing? She pointed her finger and zapped the screaming machine into silence.

As she lowered her head back down to her pillow, Sabrina remembered why she was awake so early—she hadn't done all of her homework! She bolted upright again, this time prying open her eyelids. Darkness or no darkness, she had to wake up and finish that report for geography. It was about tectonic plates, which slipped her mind a lot more easily than they slipped around the earth.

"School has only been in session for a week,"

she groused as she stumbled out of bed and grabbed her robe. "That's too soon to have homework. On a Monday, too."

She looked around for Salem and found it odd that he wasn't underfoot as usual. Oh, well, the cat would appear as soon as she reached the kitchen. He always showed up whenever anyone was in the kitchen.

Sabrina clomped wearily down the stairs and turned on the hall light. A pleasant smell wafted from the kitchen. It wasn't the usual somebody-forgot-to-do-the-dishes or to-clean-the-litter-box smell; this scent was clean and aromatic.

When she reached the kitchen and turned on the lights, Sabrina had to shield her eyes from the bright glare. The sink, the refrigerator—everything was sparkling! With her eyes half shut she stumbled around, looking for her books. Then she remembered she had left them on the counter.

She felt around, found a sheaf of papers, and squinted at them. "Oh, that's nice. It's my report—all done and neatly printed out." With a big smile, Sabrina laid the papers down on the counter and turned to go back to bed.

"I must have woken up in the middle of the night and done this stuff," she told herself.

Yeah, right, muttered her inner voice.

Sabrina yawned. "Okay, who am I going to believe? The voice that's talking out loud or the one that's only talking in my head?" She paused to make a decision, then made one. "Homework is done—somehow—so it's time to go back to bed."

But there was that troubling sweet aroma, and the chrome in their kitchen was gleaming as it never had before.

Reluctantly, Sabrina opened her eyes and took a good look around the kitchen. The first thing she saw a vase of fresh flowers. Then she screamed, "Aunt Hilda! Aunt Zelda!"

With a flurry of silk and feather boas, her two eccentric aunts came swooping down the stairs. Their hair was frightful, and so was Aunt Hilda's green beauty mask.

"We've been robbed!" shouted Sabrina.

Aunt Zelda rushed over to her laptop computer, which sat in its usual spot on the kitchen table. Aunt Hilda ran to inspect the silverware, which was all clean and neatly stacked, not in its usual mixed-up jumble in the drawer.

"What's been stolen?" asked Zelda.

"The mess!" Sabrina shook her head, realizing how silly that sounded. "We weren't robbed, exactly, but we have had intruders. Somebody came in and left these flowers. He also cleaned the kitchen and did my homework."

Zelda grinned with delight as she studied the screen of her laptop computer. "He also balanced my checkbook and did this month's household budget! Hilda, you're still spending too much for hair dye."

But Aunt Hilda wasn't paying any attention. She walked around the kitchen peering into corners and behind furniture. She waved a shiny fork in the air. "This silver hasn't been polished this well in centuries. I think we have a hobby."

Sabrina shook her head. "Thanks, but I don't want to polish silverware for a hobby."

"Not that kind of hobby," said Zelda with concern. "A hobgoblin."

"What's that?" asked Sabrina, certain it was bad.

"A hobgoblin is a household spirit who protects the home and does useful chores in the middle of the night," explained Zelda. "He just picks a witch's house and moves in."

Sabrina tossed her blond hair. "You mean this hobgoblin is going to come in every night and clean the house, do my homework, wash the dishes, and do whatever else has to be done? You go, Hobgoblin!"

"Oh, it sounds great," Hilda said with a frown. "As long as you're grateful and don't make him mad. If a hobgoblin gets mad at you, he can cause a lot of damage. No witch can match one for pure magical fury. Although hobgoblins are usually invisible, they can appear to be anyone they want."

"If you thank them enough, sometimes they'll go away," said Zelda helpfully.

"Oh, thank you, thank you, thank you!" cooed Hilda.

"No, wait!" said Sabrina, cupping her aunt's mouth. "Let's have a little patience, Aunt Hilda. I mean, what has this poor hobgoblin done to be banned from our house so soon? Besides, how do we know it *was* a hobgoblin? We have some very strange relatives who might have come in here and left us these flowers."

"She has a point," said Aunt Zelda. "Besides, trying to get rid of the hobgoblin so quickly might tick him off. And he's a great accountant."

"I can see my reflection in this silverware," muttered Hilda glumly. "I warn you—a hobgoblin can make witches lazy. Some of them can even forget how to cast spells, let alone unplug the garbage disposal."

"And you have to feed a hobby," added Aunt Zelda. "But they'll eat almost anything."

"Sounds like Salem. Where is that mangy cat, anyway?" Sabrina looked around, then covered her mouth with one hand, her eyes widening in horror. "You don't suppose ... Could the hobgoblin have turned Salem back into a warlock?"

"No, they like to do mundane things, like washing pots and pans," answered Hilda. "Cats have instincts that we don't have, and Salem might have spotted him first. He's probably hiding under a bed somewhere."

Hilda snapped her fingers and—*poof!*—a

black cat appeared on the kitchen counter. Salem looked plumper than usual, with his sleek fur all shampooed and blow-dried and two cute little yellow ribbons tied behind his ears. He smelled as if a whole bottle of perfume had been dumped on him, and he had never looked more embarrassed in his life.

"I'm so mortified!" he wailed. "I tried to jump out the window and end it all, but I kept landing on my *feet!*"

Despite her best intentions, Sabrina laughed out loud, and so did her aunts. "Salem, what happened to you?" she asked.

"A ferocious ghost grabbed me, threw me in the bathtub, shampooed me, and gave me a blow-dry. He completely violated my privacy, and I demand to *sue* that ghost!"

"It wasn't a ghost," said Hilda. "It was a hobgoblin. At least that's what we think."

"Then I'll *sue* that hobgoblin," declared Salem. "What's his address?"

"He lives here," answered Sabrina. "And he was only doing chores that needed doing. In your case, double."

Salem scowled darkly. "Do you recall those immortal words, 'No good deed goes unpunished'?"

"If he shows up again, that means he's decided to stay," said Hilda. "We'll know for sure tomorrow morning."

Sabrina clapped her hands together. "As long as we're up and the kitchen is totally clean, let's make it a mess again! Anyone for French toast?"

"What about your homework, which you now have to do on your own?" said Aunt Zelda.

The teenager frowned. "Right, like you're going to redo your checking account and the budget?"

"Well, I'm going to double-check them," said Zelda, quickly sitting at her computer.

"Then I'll double-check my homework," countered Sabrina. "Aunt Hilda, will you please make the French toast?"

"Wait!" roared Salem. "Before you do anything else, will somebody please remove these bows from my ears?" He sobbed pathetically.

Sabrina whistled cheerfully as she strolled along the sidewalk toward school. Summer finally seemed to be over, and for the first time she noticed the dry, crackling chill of autumn. The scent of cinnamon and nutmeg wafted from an open window, while pine logs burned aromatically in a nearby fireplace.

A cool breeze rustled through the trees, making the yellow leaves shimmer like golden medallions. By next week, Sabrina, knew, those leaves would be flaming red and collecting in piles on the ground.

With delight, Sabrina realized that she would

be early to school for the first time since . . . since she couldn't remember. But that didn't matter—she was early! Despite her aunts' gloomy mutterings, she could get used to having a hobgoblin around to make life easier.

Hardly seeing a soul, Sabrina walked up the old gray steps and entered Westbridge High School. What did people do at a high school before classes started? Curious to find out, Sabrina snooped around the halls.

Hmmm, there was Mr. Kraft, the vice-principal. He was very efficiently tearing down all the signs for student dances, the Drama Club, the Computer Club, the marching band, the chorus, and every other extracurricular activity.

She walked up behind him and asked cheerfully, "What are you doing?"

Mr. Kraft jumped about six feet, then whirled around. "Sabrina Spellman?" he asked in amazement. He cleaned his glasses and checked his watch. "It's really *you*—at school half an hour early! Did you forget to set your clock back when daylight saving time ended?"

"No, I'm just early. What are you doing?"

"Removing all the signs for extracurricular activities," he answered, grabbing the one for the Chess Club.

"I can see that, but why?"

"Because we're not going to have all that stuff anymore," the vice-principal answered with a satisfied smile. "It's a new school year, and you know what *that* means."

"More sawdust in the meat loaf?"

"Besides that, a new school year always means less money from the school board. We would hit up the PTA, but they're still paying off expenses from last year. We've got so little money that we need to choose between having textbooks and teachers, or a school dance."

"I vote for the school dance," said Sabrina, thinking he was joking.

Kraft smiled. "Luckily, Miss Spellman, I set the priorities around here, not you." He walked over to the bulletin board and yanked down the sign-up sheet for the Camera Club.

"You're serious!" exclaimed Sabrina in shock. "But school can't be just about . . . *school!*"

"Sorry." He yanked down the sign-up sheet for the Pep Club.

"Not the Pep Club!" she wailed. "What will our school do without *pep?* We've always had pep."

"I think we can do with a little less pep." Kraft's hand hesitated at the sign-up sheet for cheerleading, and Sabrina knew he was messing with one of the sacred clubs. Sure, he had the guts to yank the Pep Club, but did he have the guts to shut down the cheerleaders?

"Oh, what the heck." With a trembling hand, Mr. Kraft tore down the sheet for the cheerleaders.

"Now you've done it," Sabrina warned darkly.

"I've seen this year's budget, and you haven't. There's *no money.* We'll keep the football team . . . for now." He turned and marched down the hall.

Sabrina ran to keep up. "Hey, can't we do something to raise funds? What do you call those things?"

"Fund-raisers." Kraft stopped and laughed out loud. "The students are already selling flowers, candy, cookies, popcorn, books, magazines, and lightbulbs. The parents are tapped out—they haven't got a dime left. If you can come up with a brand-new fund-raiser we haven't tried, I'll listen. Until then, why don't you stir up some pep?"

Still chuckling and shaking his head, Mr. Kraft walked away. Desperate, Sabrina looked around the hallway and saw that students were starting to trickle in. Like most teens, they didn't see anything but each other, and they walked right past the empty bulletin boards.

She saw her friend Valerie heading to her locker, and she charged after her. "Val, the Science Club, the school newspaper, the Pep Club— they're all gone!"

Valerie gaped at her. "What are you talking about?"

"And you're a cheerleader, too," said Sabrina, flapping her arms. "Even the pom-poms got the axe." She quickly told her friend about what she had caught Mr. Kraft doing and why.

Valerie was aghast. "He can't do that. We'll . . . we'll—"

"What will we do?" asked Sabrina eagerly.

"We'll sell more cookies!"

Sabrina shook her head, knowing that Valerie was not exactly a mover and shaker of high school life. But the person who fit that description had just rounded the corner, followed by a squad of chattering girls.

"Libby!" cried Sabrina, rushing over to her dark-haired nemesis. "You're looking very, uh . . . peppy this morning."

"It's Monday morning," grumbled Libby. "That's too early in the week for you to give me grief. Come back on Wednesday."

"But there's a real problem. Did you notice that there's no sign-up sheet for cheerleading?"

"You're not going to try out for cheerleader again, are you?" asked Libby with mock horror. "I don't think the school could survive such embarrassment again."

"Look around, Libby. There is no cheerleading squad! Mr. Kraft canceled it, along with every other extracurricular activity." In a rush, she told Libby what had happened, while several other students gathered around to hear the tale of woe.

"He can't do that!" declared Libby. "The Pep Club, okay, that's only plain-looking girls. But the cheerleading squad has all the *pretty* girls!"

"I knew this would offend your sense of fairness," said Sabrina.

"I'm going to go set him straight," vowed Libby, marching off toward the vice-principal's office. "He can't mess with the cheerleaders."

Valerie sidled up to Sabrina and said, "That's like fighting fire with gasoline."

"Libby and Mr. Kraft have been tight before," replied Sabrina. "If anyone can get him to change his mind, it will be Libby."

Mrs. Quick suddenly crossed in front of them, bustling to someplace or another, her squinched-up face buried in test papers. Sabrina rushed after her.

"Mrs. Quick!" she called, skidding to a stop behind the gangly teacher. "Have you heard what happened to the Drama Club?"

"I thought it was right where I left it."

"No, Mr. Kraft canceled it, along with every other extracurricular activity. He says there's no money."

"Well, of course there's no money," sniffed Mrs. Quick. "But that's never stopped us before. If we can't do this season's play, *Picnic*, I'll be very mad."

"Didn't we do *Picnic* two years ago?" asked Sabrina with a frown.

Mrs. Quick stared off into the distance, smiling wistfully. "Yes, but it's such a nice play. It has so many pretty summer dresses, a small-town atmosphere . . . and a nice young man with his shirt off."

"Well, Mr. Kraft has canceled the picnic this year." Once again, Sabrina explained what had happened, and Mrs. Quick crossed her arms and scowled in anger.

"I'll reason with him." Looking determined, the teacher bustled off toward Mr. Kraft's office.

"That should fix it," Valerie assured Sabrina. "Good job."

A minute later terrible feedback squealed over the public-address system, and Mr. Kraft cleared his throat. "Attention, all students and faculty. It doesn't matter *who* you send down to my office, all extracurricular clubs have been canceled due to lack of funds."

"Aw!" said most of the students in the hallway.

Some bickering sounded over the speaker, and Mr. Kraft grumbled. "All right. Mrs. Quick has suggested a compromise. We'll all meet after school in the lunchroom to discuss new fund-raising possibilities. But I don't hold much hope. School has only been in session for a week, and the parents refuse to buy anything else that their kids are selling."

"The parents are always broke," muttered Valerie. "We need to hit up the people who have the money—the kids."

Sabrina nodded thoughtfully. "That's a great idea! We have to find something that will appeal to teenagers and people going out on a date. But what?"

As the hallways erupted with a roar of conversation, Sabrina heard the familiar voice of Harvey Kinkle, shouting over the din. "Hey, Sabrina! What are you doing for Halloween?"

Halloween? The teenage witch waved to her boyfriend, and Harvey fought his way through the crowd to reach her side. When he got there, she gave him a brazen kiss, and he blinked at her with surprise. "Why'd you do that?"

"Because you gave me a dynamite idea how to save the school year." Sabrina grinned and rubbed her hands together.

Chapter 2

After school, about a hundred students gathered in the lunchroom of Westbridge High, and they were all talking at once. It was like lunchtime, thought Sabrina, only with no food. Mr. Kraft was presiding over this unruly group, under the watchful eye of Mrs. Quick. Her stern expression made it clear that she would fight to save the Drama Club, the Pep Club, and all the other extracurricular activities.

Mr. Kraft smiled obsequiously into the microphone, and his voice boomed across the crowded room. "Settle down, everyone. *You* wanted to be here, not me."

After their voices died down, he continued, "We are gathered here to dream up yet another fund-raiser for Westbridge High. But I warn you, your parents and neighbors are already complaining about all the fund-raisers we have now. So does anyone have any suggestions?"

Bobby Hubert jumped to his feet. "What about setting up an offshore gambling empire? We could offer cyberbingo!"

Mr. Kraft raised a cautionary finger. "Gambling is against school policy, and I don't think we should do anything that will get us arrested and thrown in jail. At least not the teachers."

"Okay," said Bobby. "Then why don't the cheerleaders do a bikini car wash?"

"Yeah!" shouted many of the boys in the audience, including Harvey.

Libby crossed her arms and grumbled, "In your dreams."

Mrs. Quick jumped to her feet and took over the microphone. "Let's make some intelligent suggestions, shall we? If we can't think of a fund-raiser that's new and different, we'll have to forgo all those activities that you children love so much."

Sabrina looked around the room at the blank, hopeless faces. She had planned to wait until other ideas had been discussed, but it didn't look as if there were going to be any other ideas. She raised her hand hesitantly.

"Yes, Miss Spellman," said Mrs. Quick with a hopeless sigh.

Sabrina rose to her feet and gave the audience a confident smile. "Halloween is coming up soon, and everyone makes money off Halloween. Look at all the Halloween books and stuff. It's the second biggest holiday for merchandise after Christmas. I've got an idea that will make us a lot of money, but it's going to require some hard work."

"Pray tell, what is it?" asked Mr. Kraft.

"For Halloween we could open a big haunted house!" Sabrina held out her hands majestically, as if envisioning a grand plan. "We'll have a fun house, a maze, special effects, and cool scenes with monsters and stuff! We can advertise it all over town, and we'll charge admission."

She paused, but nobody threw spit wads at her or told her to shut up. So she went on, "We can also sell candy, pumpkins, and other stuff at rip-off prices. Other organizations do this, and they make good money. We can open the haunted house for three or four weekends, running Friday and Saturday nights."

Mr. Kraft and Mrs. Quick blinked at each other, startled by her excellent suggestion. Sabrina held her breath, waiting for somebody to give a good reason why it couldn't be done, but no one said anything. Libby was thinking hard, trying to come up with an objection, but she couldn't think of one either.

A smile spread across Mrs. Quick's face. "You know, building the props and sets, playing the monsters—that would be good experience for the Drama Club. It's just the kind of thing we *should* be doing."

At once everyone began to talk excitedly about the haunted house. Sabrina beamed with pride over the fact that everyone was taking her idea so seriously.

Mr. Kraft pulled a calculator from his pocket and started punching figures into it. "If we had five hundred customers each night, at five dollars a head, we would collect five thousand dollars a weekend! If we stayed open for three weekends, we'd make fifteen thousand dollars. Even if we had to spend half of that for expenses, we would still have enough money to support all of the extracurricular activities."

"And that's not even counting the treats at rip-off prices!" added Valerie.

Suddenly Mr. Kraft pulled a Jekyll and Hyde—his smile morphed into a dour frown. "Lumber and special effects are expensive. We could *lose* money if we aren't careful. I'm not sure it's worth the risk."

"First things first," said Mrs. Quick resolutely. "We really can't decide to create a haunted house until we find a suitable place for it."

"What about the school gym?" asked Libby.

Mr. Kraft shook his head vigorously and grabbed the microphone. "No, we can't disrupt phys ed classes and basketball practice. I guess we just can't offer a haunted house. So sorry, students—go back to your lives!"

"Nonsense," scoffed Mrs. Quick, grabbing

back the microphone. "We just need to find a big building we can take over for several weeks and mess up as much as we want. An old barn or an empty warehouse would be good. Does anybody know of any vacant buildings large enough for our purpose?"

Slowly Harvey raised his hand. "I know of a place. It's the old baby-carriage factory downtown. The new owners have hired my dad to exterminate the place before they remodel, but I don't think they're going to start for a couple of months. Maybe they would let us use it."

Mr. Kraft looked doubtful. "Is this factory in good condition? The school board frowns on students getting killed in industrial accidents."

"Does it have huge vats full of molten metal?" asked Bobby Hubert. "We could do *Terminator II!*"

"Yeah! Yeah!" echoed everyone in the room, talking at once and suggesting their favorite movie scenes. "*Nightmare on Elm Street!*" shouted another. "Is there a furnace?"

"Quiet down!" snapped Mrs. Quick. "Let Harvey talk."

Harvey gave a modest shrug, looking sheepish and cute. "The factory is mostly empty, but it's already kind of spooky. We'll have to do lots of cleaning, but I don't think the owners will mind that. Uh, there is one more thing. . . ."

He frowned hesitantly, then went on, "The factory is said to be haunted by a *real* ghost."

19

There were nervous chuckles, and Mrs. Quick laughed out loud. "Even better! We'll put that in all the ads and publicity. Can you find some details about this ghost?"

"Sure," said Harvey. "I'll ask the owners."

"All right!" Mrs. Quick sounded like a cheerleader. "There's no business like show business! This will be just like putting on a play, so there is a lot of work to be done. Sabrina, since this was your idea, I'm sure you'll want to chair the haunted house committee."

"What?" shrieked Sabrina. "But I wasn't—"

"And we need a good name for it," declared Mrs. Quick. "What do you call a haunted house inside a factory?"

"Insanity," muttered Mr. Kraft.

Mrs. Quick shook her head. "Halloween Insanity? That's good, but not quite right. Something with a more industrial feel."

"I know!" chirped Valerie. "The Halloween Machine!"

"The Halloween Machine," echoed Mrs. Quick, nodding with approval. "I believe we have our name. All in favor of calling it the Halloween Machine, raise your hand!"

A hundred hands shot up, even Libby's, and Valerie beamed with excitement at having suggested the name.

Sabrina wanted to freeze the action and back up to that moment when she had been selected to chair the committee, which sounded like a lot of responsibility and work. But then she remembered that she had help at home—their new hobgoblin. Maybe she shouldn't worry about doing a little extra work.

"We need someone to take charge of publicity and advertising." Mrs. Quick looked at Valerie. "You can do it, with your experience on the school newspaper."

"Sure!" Valerie answered excitedly. She turned to Sabrina and gushed. "Isn't this going to be fun?"

"I hope so." Sabrina was still partly on the side of Mr. Kraft, who looked doubtful about this whole enterprise. Even though it had been her idea, she could see the potential problems . . . and how much work it was going to be.

Mrs. Quick was hurriedly scribbling notes. "Everyone is on the cleaning committee, and we also need people for set construction, costumes, lights, sound, and transportation."

"Count me in for construction," said Harvey. Lots of other kids also volunteered to pound nails and paint sets, and Harvey motioned for them to gather around him. Sabrina couldn't believe it— all over the lunchroom, the students broke up into small groups, trying to find other souls who wanted to sew costumes, put together the sound system, and cart stuff in their trucks. Valerie gathered a bunch of the school newspaper people to handle advertising.

Hey, thought Sabrina, *with all these people to help me, plus the hobgoblin, this will be easy!*

She didn't see Mr. Kraft slither up to her until it was too late. Since other people were watching them, he gave her an insincere smile and whispered, "Sabrina, this had better come off without a hitch. If things go wrong and we lose money, I'll never forget whose idea this was. There will be only one after-school activity for you—detention."

Sabrina gulped and looked for a way to escape, but she wasn't saved until Mrs. Quick squeezed between them. "Sabrina, you and Harvey should come with me to talk to the owners and check out this building. Mr. Kraft, you can arrange for insurance, building permits, and the fire marshal. That sounds like a fun job for you!"

"Oh, just jolly," he sneered. "Where are we going to get the money to buy insurance and supplies and to rent equipment?"

"Corporate sponsors!" answered Mrs. Quick. "All those businesses we talk into buying ads in the football program and the yearbook. I think we can raise a few hundred dollars in seed money, and maybe the businesses will donate materials, too. Sabrina, that will be your next job."

"*My* job?" asked Sabrina. "I have to do fundraising for the fund-raiser?"

"That's life in the arts," said Mrs. Quick dramatically. She turned to address everyone, and her sharp voice cut through the din in the lunchroom. "Listen up, children! Once we commit to doing this, there's no turning back, no bailing out. Everyone in this room has to go out and recruit more workers, plus merchants who can donate materials to the cause.

"I'll call some other drama teachers and get some advice on making a haunted house. The rest of you can start thinking about skits and monsters!"

Delighted laughter broke out in the lunchroom, as Sabrina's idea took on a life of its own, sort of like the Frankenstein monster. Somehow, just because she had come up with this crazy notion, she was in charge of the haunted house, or at least second-in-command to Mrs. Quick.

Sabrina turned to look at Mr. Kraft, and he arched an eyebrow at her. He was the only one, besides her, who looked properly worried.

"Isn't it great?" asked Valerie. "You brought the whole school together in one fund-raiser—it's all because of *you!*"

"Yeah," agreed Sabrina with a wan smile.

To say that the old baby-carriage factory was spooky was an understatement. When Sabrina stepped out of Mrs. Quick's car, she saw a gigantic cube built of aged red bricks and covered with gnarly black vines. There were two rows of windows just under the rusted metal roof, and all of them were broken. A giant smokestack stood silent, looming over the old building like a watchful guard tower.

The neighborhood was not exactly downtown, as Harvey had said; it was south of downtown in an old industrial area near the railroad tracks. Sabrina decided that she wouldn't want to be alone here after dark, and she noticed that the clouds were already turning into chocolate swirls. It would be dark very soon.

Harvey stepped closer to her, as if sensing her discomfort, and Mrs. Quick hurriedly locked her car doors. At least the parking lot was large— large enough for lots of cars, hayrides, and food booths. On one side of the building was a weathered painting of an old-fashioned baby carriage, which looked weird, like a ghostly hearse.

"Well, at least we don't have to decorate the outside," said Sabrina, trying to sound cheerful.

"Oh, I don't know," replied Mrs. Quick thoughtfully. "A few ghosts and skeletons hanging among the vines would add a nice touch. We'll have to do something about those broken windows, too."

"Maybe we can cover them up with banners," said Harvey. "I hope there's an easy way to get to them." He walked cautiously toward a metal door that looked as if it hadn't been opened for fifty years. "I called my dad, and he said the caretaker would meet us here at the east door."

"A deserted factory has a caretaker?" asked Sabrina.

"Well, they still have to do maintenance and stuff." Harvey removed his hand from the doorknob, and it was covered with dirt. He wiped it sheepishly on his pants and said, "Maybe he's not here very much."

Mrs. Quick tried the doorknob, and she also found it locked. When she pounded forcefully on the metal door, the sound echoed like a prisoner pounding on the bars of his cell. With a terrible flapping, a flock of pigeons bolted from one of the broken windows, causing Mrs. Quick to shriek and duck for cover. Sabrina aimed her finger in case the birds tried to dive-bomb them, but they soared over the roof and were gone.

Mrs. Quick cleared her throat and smoothed out her dress. "Yes, indeed, we have to do something about those windows. Now, I wonder where—"

The door suddenly creaked open, causing her to jump back in alarm. Harvey stepped forward just as a man in overalls stepped out. He was wearing thick glasses, and he squinted suspiciously at all three of them. To Sabrina, he looked like someone's grumpy grandfather.

"Are you the folks I'm supposed to let in?" he asked. "The ones Mr. McGibbons called about?"

"That would be us," answered Mrs. Quick, sounding huffy over the scare she had gotten. "And you would be . . . ?"

"Charlie Haynes, the caretaker of this place."

Mrs. Quick quickly introduced the three of them and explained the reason for their visit. "So you see," she concluded, "Mr. McGibbons has given us permission to use this building for our fund-raiser. If you will be so kind as to show us around, we'll decide what we need to do next."

Charlie scratched his grizzled chin. "If that's what the owner wants, that's what I'll do, all right. But *he* won't like it."

"We've already got Mr. McGibbons's permission," insisted Mrs. Quick.

"I don't mean him." The caretaker leaned forward and whispered, "I mean the haunt."

Sabrina laughed nervously. "The haunt."

"That's what we called them back in the hills," answered the old man, studying the silent catwalks. "A haunt is a ghost, a poltergeist . . . a whatchamacallit."

"That's just an old story, right?" said Sabrina with a nervous laugh. "Something to scare the trespassers away."

"There ain't no story that I know of," answered Charlie. "But there's *something* up there. He was there even before we closed."

Just as all three of them were waiting breathlessly for more of the story, the caretaker waved them off. "But you folks ain't interested in that. You want to look around, see what you can do with this old dump."

He held the heavy door open for them to enter; then he led the way with his flashlight. They entered what looked like a huge dark cavern, and Sabrina expected bats to dive toward their heads. She couldn't see much, but what she saw was plenty spooky. Maybe they could charge admission to the factory just the way it was.

"Aren't there any lights?" asked Mrs. Quick worriedly.

"Sure, but it's expensive to light this place up," Charlie explained. "I only use a flashlight, except in my office in the back."

Mrs. Quick brushed a cobweb out of her face and stiffened her back. "I refuse to take one more step until you turn on some lights."

"Oh, all right, but *he* won't like it." Still grumbling, the caretaker shuffled off."

After he was gone, Harvey whispered, "I say we put a hump on Charlie and make him play Igor."

"I heard that!" shouted a distant voice. A moment later bright floodlights illuminated the cavernous building.

There wasn't much to see—just a huge room with a ceiling about three stories high. There were a few remnants from when the place had been a working factory. Hanging from the ceiling were chains and pulleys, and against the wall were work pits, sooty kilns, and chipped sinks. A narrow catwalk ran the length of the building under the broken windows, and there were small doors in the back. Sabrina figured they led to the offices and rest rooms.

A fine layer of dust coated the cement floor, but there wasn't much junk lying around. The building looked as if it would clean up nicely, thought Sabrina. They would probably leave the kilns alone, because they looked like eerie black furnaces. Maybe they could do a tribute to Freddy Krueger.

Mrs. Quick nodded with satisfaction. "Yes, yes, this will do nicely. We'll have to build narrow corridors, platforms, and small rooms for the maze. But we have a lot to work with."

Sabrina heard footsteps and turned to see Charlie Haynes shuffling toward them. "You folks want to make this place haunted?"

They all nodded.

"But it's already haunted." Charlie gazed upward toward the spooky catwalks and broken windows.

"But it's not a fund-raiser for the school yet," sniffed Mrs. Quick. "Remember, we have the owners' permission."

"I know, but you don't have *his* permission," warned Charlie.

Mrs. Quick crossed her arms and gazed at the old man as if he were a student who had given a dumb answer. "What exactly does this ghost of yours do?"

"Just about whatever he wants to do. If you're lucky, he'll just steal a tool every now and then."

"That reminds me," said Mrs. Quick, making a note on her pad. "We need bins to keep our tools, props, and costumes in. Ghost or no ghost, I don't want anything getting lost."

Harvey looked at the caretaker. "You know, Charlie, whether the ghost likes it or not, this factory is going to reopen in a few months."

"Yes," answered the caretaker, adjusting his glasses. "It'll be interesting to see how he gets along with the company. Say, if we're going to turn the electricity and heat on full-time again, I've got a lot of work to do. When are you folks going to get started?"

"Tomorrow after school," answered Mrs. Quick.

"I'll be here, and I'll have a key made for you." Charlie Haynes scurried off, kicking up a curtain of dust that swirled through the air after him.

"Thank you!" called Sabrina.

They walked around, discussing all the things they could do with the huge empty space. Finally, Sabrina looked up and saw only darkness through the high broken windows, and she shivered. "It's getting late," she said. "Maybe we can think up more gruesome stuff tomorrow."

"You're right," said Mrs. Quick. "Just let me make a couple more notes." She searched her pockets, then her purse, but she seemed to be missing something.

"That's odd," she said. "I just had my notebook. . . . Now, what did I do with it?"

Sabrina and Harvey looked around, but they couldn't spot the notebook on the dusty floor. Since night had fallen, there were dark corners and eerie pools of shadow in the old factory. If the teacher had dropped her notebook, it could be anywhere in the huge room.

"Well, darn it!" snapped Mrs. Quick. "I can't imagine what happened to that notebook."

They heard a fluttering sound, and all three of them ducked, expecting pigeons to swoop toward their heads. Then Sabrina saw it—a small notebook fluttering down from the shadows. With a clap, it landed at Mrs. Quick's feet, making her jump back.

Harvey moved closer to Sabrina; she couldn't tell if it was for *her* protection or *his*. "Is that it?" he asked with a gulp.

Mrs. Quick gingerly picked up the notebook, acting as if it might explode in her hand. "Okay, we've got it. Now let's get out of here!"

The three of them raced each other to the door.

Chapter 3

When Mrs. Quick dropped Sabrina off at her house, it was dark and almost eight o'clock. She hurried through the front door and into kitchen, where she found Aunt Hilda just hanging up the phone.

"Oh, you're home," said Hilda with relief. She picked up a sheaf of papers and began to read them. "There are messages for you from the publicity committee, the transportation committee, and the construction committee. Did you get elected president and not tell anyone?"

Sabrina grinned with pride. "No, but I came up with a cool idea to save all the after-school programs. We're going to make a haunted house and charge admission. It'll be the greatest fund-raiser in the history of Westbridge High!"

Zelda walked through the kitchen, carrying the vase of flowers the hobgoblin had left. "As long as we don't have to buy any cookies, popcorn, magazines, or lightbulbs." She placed the vase in the sink and refilled it.

"No, none of that." Sabrina explained the plan and how she had been made the chairperson of the haunted house project.

"That's a big job," said Zelda with concern. "Are you sure you can do all that, plus keep up with your schoolwork and your witch studies?"

"Sure," said Sabrina. "I'll just leave the paperwork out at night for the hobgoblin to do."

Hilda frowned. "Yes, and what if the hobgoblin decides to leave one day?"

"Don't worry, I've got ten committees and a hundred people working for me." Sabrina wandered over to the refrigerator and looked inside. "What's for dinner?"

"An excellent question," said a droll male voice. Salem leaped onto the kitchen counter and swished his tail expectantly. "What *is* for dinner?"

"Oh, come on, Salem, I fed you an hour ago," said Aunt Hilda.

"Where did you put the food?" asked the cat.

"In your dish."

The black cat jumped down to the floor and peered at his food dish, which was quite empty. "I know this isn't a first-class restaurant, but these portions are *very* small."

"Come on, Salem," muttered Hilda, "you're not going to trick me into feeding you twice."

"Isn't it bad enough that I have to eat cat food?" wailed the cat. "You can't let me starve! You wouldn't even do that to a *dog*."

"You're on a diet," Aunt Zelda reminded him.

"I'm on a diet," grumbled the cat, "not a hunger strike."

Hilda scratched her head in puzzlement. "Hmmm, I wonder . . . Let me try an experiment."

She reached into the cupboard and took out a can of cat food, which she opened with the can opener.

"Ah, music to my ears," said Salem, cocking his head.

"But you're not allowed to eat any of this," answered Hilda. She picked up his bowl and began to spoon food into it.

"Not eat any of it?" asked Salem with a gasp. "Is the purpose of this experiment to see how long it takes for me to beg? Look at me . . . I'm begging! I'm begging!" He rolled over on his back and pretended to be dead.

"Just stay away from the food for a moment." Hilda set his dish on the floor, and they all stood around, looking at it.

"This is better than watching TV," said Salem. "In fact, if this were on TV, it would be my favorite program."

"Sshh," warned Hilda. "Something is happening."

"Yes, I'm dying of hunger!" groaned the cat.

Now Sabrina looked more closely at the bowl of gray cat food. Little by little it was disappearing. After a few seconds, the food was gone.

"I don't know how you did that," said Salem, "but I wish you would stop it."

"I didn't do it," said Hilda with a frown. "I think we found out what the hobgoblin likes to eat."

"Cat food?" asked Sabrina with surprise.

"Can't you feed him a T-bone steak?" muttered Salem.

"I doubt if he would eat it," said Zelda. "Hobgoblins are very particular, once they find something they like."

"Well, then, feed *me* the T-bone steak," suggested Salem. "Give him the cat food, with my blessings."

"Does he like everything cats like?" asked Sabrina.

"Let's see." Hilda pointed her finger at Salem's empty bowl, and it promptly filled up with milk. An invisible tongue began to lap at the milk, and a few seconds later it was all gone.

"Wow, this is the best dinner I never had," Salem grumbled.

"That is so weird," said Sabrina. "Maybe it's not the food but Salem's bowl that he likes."

"If he likes my bowl, he's going to *love* my litter box," said the cat. "Maybe he'll eat that, too."

Zelda put her hands on her hips and frowned. "What are we going to do about this?"

"The solution is simple," answered Salem. "From now on, I'll eat people food from people plates, and you can start buying cheap cat food."

"We do buy cheap cat food," Hilda answered.

"I knew it!" Salem began to weep pitifully at the injustice of it all.

Hilda got another bowl from the cupboard, and another can of cat food. "You shouldn't eat people food; it's not good for you."

The cat shook his head. "If it's not good for your pet, why is it good for *you?* Who made up that stupid rule, anyway? When I'm dictator of the world, the cats will eat whatever they want, and we'll feed people only what's good for them. No more french fries and chocolate éclairs—only bran flakes and broccoli."

"Mmmm," said Zelda. "A chocolate éclair sounds good." She pointed her finger, and a whole plate of them appeared on the kitchen counter.

"At last, a proper dinner," said Salem, edging toward the plate of éclairs.

Hilda grabbed the cat before he got halfway there. "I'll prepare a fresh bowl of food for you, and I'll feed you on the back porch."

"Oh, joy—kicked out of my own house," grumbled Salem. "Hobgoblin, you'd better watch your back!"

After they left, Sabrina laughed nervously. "Don't listen to him, Mr. Hobgoblin. He's just a cat. We appreciate you. By the way, do you do dry cleaning?"

Aunt Zelda smiled. "You don't need to tell a hobgoblin what needs to be done; he knows instinctively."

"Cool." Sabrina grabbed an éclair and her stack of messages. "I'd better return all these calls. You're a businesswoman, Aunt Zelda. Do you have any advice on how we should plan this fund-raiser?"

"You need publicity, and lots of it. But the best kind of publicity is the free kind. See if you can get the local newspapers and radio and TV stations to cover your grand opening."

"That's a great idea, thanks." Munching her éclair, Sabrina charged up the stairs to her room.

This is easy, she thought. *All I have to do is talk on the phone and tell people what to do. I can do that!*

The next morning, Sabrina woke up and found her most stylish outfit folded over her chair, ready to wear. Clothes that had been lying on the floor of the laundry room were now clean, pressed, and hanging neatly in her closet. On her desk was a bunch of notes for the haunted house, all typed up and organized.

"Wow!" she said. "Thank you, Hobgoblin."

After getting dressed, she walked downstairs and found the kitchen spotless and shiny, as expected. Delicious-smelling bacon and eggs were cooking, and toast popped out of the toaster, although no one was around. Sabrina grabbed a plate and loaded up her breakfast, again thanking her invisible servant.

While Sabrina ate breakfast, she heard a pitiful scratching at the back door. Curious, she got up and opened the door. A bedraggled black cat sat there on the porch. He was covered with dirt and leaves. She almost didn't recognize him . . . until he talked.

"Is it safe to come in?" asked Salem, shivering pathetically.

"Sure. What happened to you?"

"I was reduced to sleeping under the house . . . in the crawl space."

"Like most cats," remarked Sabrina.

"I'm not most cats," said Salem haughtily as he strutted into the room. "At least I didn't get a bath last night."

Sabrina wrinkled her nose. "Yeah, I can tell that. But you could have slept inside."

"Are you kidding?" asked the cat. "With that noisy hobgoblin tromping around all night! Now that I eat outside, and sleep outside, I might as well be an alley cat. I would ask for some food, but I figure *he* ate it all."

Sabrina opened the cupboard, and it was

stocked with a fresh supply of cat food, plus a lot of people food. "Actually, it looks as if he went shopping for us."

The cat snorted. "I suppose that next he'll do the dry cleaning."

"I'm afraid he already did it." She opened two cans of food—one for the cat and one for the hobgoblin. Salem did not fail to notice that she filled the hobgoblin's bowl first.

He sniffed pathetically. "You know, I always thought it would be good to have another pet in the house—to take the pressure off me. But I never thought that my masters would love *him* more than they love me." Salem began to whimper.

Sabrina scoffed. "Oh, come on. We don't love the hobgoblin more than we love you. Just because he does all these amazing things for us while you . . . well, you mostly lie around and cause trouble. But we still love you."

"You don't sound very convincing," Salem said glumly. "I'll go out on the porch, where you can feed me. Then I'll curl up under the house. Maybe I'll even eat a mouse."

Sabrina laughed. "You don't eat mice."

"I couldn't even if I wanted to," complained the cat. "The hobgoblin got rid of them all! I heard the mice packing up and leaving last night. I wanted to join them, but for some reason mice don't like to travel with a cat."

"Good morning!" said a cheery voice.

Sabrina turned to see Aunt Zelda sweep into the kitchen. The stylish witch went immediately to her laptop on the kitchen table, and she smiled with satisfaction. "Why, that's wonderful!" she exclaimed. "The hobgoblin has done the quarterly tax returns for the art gallery."

"I thought we weren't going to depend on him too much," said Sabrina with a sly smile.

Zelda looked flustered. "Well, I wouldn't want to deprive him of the great pleasure of doing these small favors for us."

"By all means, let's not deprive the hobgoblin," Salem muttered. "Let's deprive the poor cat instead."

"You're hardly deprived," answered Zelda. "You brought the punishment of being a cat onto yourself. Maybe if you were more helpful around here, like the hobgoblin, you could complain; but you can't. Now go outside and eat like a good kitty."

Scowling darkly, the cat slunk off, with Sabrina trailing behind him. She heard him mutter, "I'll be the number one pet again, you wait and see."

For the second day in a row, Sabrina waltzed cheerfully into school a few minutes early. She found Mr. Kraft putting back the posters for cheerleader sign-up and Chess Club meetings, and he gave her a dour frown. He didn't need to say what he was thinking—that if the haunted house failed to make money, it would be *her* fault.

Sabrina ignored him and looked around for her friends. The first one she spotted was Valerie, just getting to her locker.

"Hi, Valerie, how's it going?" Sabrina said, charging up to her best friend.

To her surprise, Valerie whirled around and stared angrily at her. "If you didn't think I could handle the publicity, Sabrina, you should have told me. I'll be happy to let you do it ... all by yourself."

"Huh?" Sabrina gaped at her friend. "What are you talking about?" Everything had been great when she talked to Valerie on the phone last night.

"You went over my head and started calling TV stations and newspapers by yourself!" snapped her friend.

"I did?" Sabrina blinked puzzledly.

"Okay, you gave them my name as the contact, and they all called me this morning. But you could have told me what you were doing." Valerie slammed her locker shut.

"Wait a minute, I—" Sabrina started to proclaim her innocence, then she stopped in midsentence. She hadn't called anyone, but what about her helpful new assistant, the hobgoblin? It was scary to think the hobgoblin was calling people, pretending to be her. But she and Aunt Zelda had been talking about calling the news outlets, and he had overheard.

"The bad thing," said Valerie, "was that I was forced to pick an opening night out of thin air. I said October fifteenth. I hope that gives us enough time. It allows us to be open for three weekends."

"Uh, sure," said Sabrina doubtfully. "You're right—I should have told you before I made those calls. But I was just so excited, I couldn't help myself! So who's coming out to cover us?"

"The *Westbridge News,* both of the local TV stations, and three radio stations." Valerie sighed, and she stopped looking so mad. "You did a good job, Sabrina, but there's a certain order of doing things. You may be in charge of the whole thing, but *I'm* supposed to do publicity and advertising."

"I won't do it again," Sabrina assured her. Under her breath, she added, "I hope."

Valerie finally smiled. "Now *you* get to tell Mr. Kraft and Mrs. Quick that we open the Halloween Machine on October fifteenth, whether we're ready or not."

"Okay," said Sabrina with a gulp.

"And here comes Mrs. Quick," said Valerie, hurrying off to her first class.

The teacher marched straight toward Sabrina,

looking as if she had something urgent to talk about. "Sabrina, did you order the members of the transportation committee to drive to the Fieldcrest Lumberyard today?"

Sabrina cringed. "I don't know—did I?"

"We have to clean up the factory first. We're not ready to bring lumber in yet. Plus we haven't got any money to pay for lumber."

"I don't know what I was thinking," answered Sabrina, pounding her head. Of course, *she* hadn't called them—it was the hobgoblin. "But we don't have much time—we open on October fifteenth."

"Who says?"

"Uh, I do." She explained that she had called the newspaper and the TV and radio stations and that they were coming to cover the opening.

"Holy cow!" exclaimed Mrs. Quick. "You are certainly a go-getter, Sabrina. Funny, I never saw that in you before."

The teenager mustered a smile. "Well, you know . . . the early bird catches the worm!"

The first bell rang, and Mrs. Quick took a deep breath. "Well, we have a lot to do after school. You go to the factory and oversee the cleaning, and I'll try to make a deal for the lumber. I'll join you at the factory when I can."

The teacher hurried off, and Sabrina turned around to go to her own locker. Suddenly she bumped into Mr. Kraft, who had been lurking around the corner, listening to them.

He gave her an evil smile. "You're just digging yourself into a deeper hole."

"No, I'm not!" she said resolutely. "We're going to create this haunted house, and it's going to make a lot of money. You wait and see."

"I hope you're right," Mr. Kraft muttered. "And just to let you know, Miss Chairperson, the building inspector will visit the factory tomorrow to make sure it's safe. He'll inspect it again after you build your sets."

"Fine, we'll be ready!" she vowed.

"Not to mention the fire marshal and the insurance agent. A lot of people will be watching what you're doing out there."

"Fine, let them watch," said Sabrina. "But after October fifteenth they have to *pay* to get in. Gotta go!"

She quickly walked away, leaving him to think about that. Meanwhile she would have to think of a way to keep the hobgoblin working, but not so hard. She would have to be careful what she said aloud in the house. There was also the problem of the haunt in the factory—if there really was a haunt. In fact, there were a lot of problems to worry about.

But I have dozens of people and a hobgoblin working for me, thought Sabrina. *Plus I'm a witch! What could possibly go wrong?*

The Spellman household was quiet with Aunt Zelda at work, Aunt Hilda at a music class, and

Sabrina at school. Salem sat on the kitchen counter, his tail swishing back and forth as he gazed at the vase of beautiful flowers. The hobgoblin had left these flowers the night before, and the witches thought it was so sweet.

What a kiss-up, thought Salem. *Why should a powerful creature like a hobgoblin leave presents for a bunch of dippy witches? And why bother to clean up their house for them? The hobgoblin couldn't be doing this just because he was nice—he had to be after something.*

"Okay, Hobgoblin," he said, sounding like a tough cat, "I'm wise to your game. You want to move me out of here as the head pet, the family familiar. But you will find that I'm not as easy to get rid of as a bunch of mice. I *fight* to hold on to my turf. And my food."

Arching his back, the cat prowled across the kitchen counter. "They like you because you keep the house clean. Well, what if the house wasn't so clean anymore? Maybe they wouldn't like you so much."

Quite on purpose the cat bumped into the vase of flowers and knocked it off the counter. It hit the floor with a satisfying crash, scattering glass, water, and crushed flowers everywhere.

"Did *I* do that?" purred the cat. "I'm so sorry. How could I be so clumsy?"

He strolled under the cupboards, where the aunts kept jars of coffee, noodles, dried beans, spices, and other kitchen goods. One by one, the cat calmly pushed the jars to the edge of the counter.

"Bombs away!" shouted Salem as he pushed the jars off the counter and watched them smash on the floor. They made such a lovely crunching sound! Soon the kitchen floor was covered with broken pottery and glass, ground coffee, smashed noodles, scattered beans, and piles of nutmeg and pepper, all congealing in the water from the broken vase.

"What a mess," he said with disapproval. "You're not doing your job, Mr. Hobgoblin. And if you think *this* is bad, wait until you see the bathroom when I get through with it. Have you ever seen skin cream mixed with cat litter?"

Suddenly the mess on the floor began to form into neat little mounds—all by itself! The hobgoblin was back at work, trying to clean up.

"Bet I can make a mess faster than you can tidy it up!" crowed Salem. Chortling to himself, the cat jumped off the kitchen counter and dashed out of the room; he charged up the stairs and into the bathroom.

A moment later crashing sounds could be heard all over the house, followed by peals of wild laughter.

Chapter 4

Seen in the daylight after school, the old factory was less frightening and imposing, but it looked really filthy. Sabrina doubted whether they could *clean* it in time for Halloween, let alone turn it into an attraction that people would pay to see.

She knew she could use witchcraft to hurry the cleaning, but this was a project for all the kids. All of them had to do their fair share, or there was no point in it. As she had found out when Valerie got mad at her, it wasn't right to let hobgoblins and witchcraft do other people's jobs for them.

So far, they were getting great support. Almost everyone at the meeting yesterday had shown up again today, and they had recruited more people. Armed with rakes, shovels, brooms, dustpans, buckets, soap, and brushes, the cleaning crew descended upon the old factory.

The caretaker, Charlie Haynes, had installed

new lightbulbs and fired up the furnace, so the building was bright and warm inside. Charlie had been skeptical yesterday, but he seemed to enjoy all the activity today. Maybe he was just glad that he didn't have to clean the immense space himself.

He and some of the cleanup crew had started covering the broken windows with cardboard and plywood. So far, there had been no sign of the ghost.

When Mrs. Quick measured the factory floor, she looked very pleased. "It's definitely big enough!" she reported. "Almost seven thousand square feet, not counting the catwalk and offices. Now we can start drawing up plans for the maze. We have to submit blueprints to the city to get a building permit."

She clapped her hands. "All right, everyone, let's get back to work!"

With good humor and thumping music from a portable CD player, the teens dug into the cobwebs, dust, and debris. They began filling trash bags, which they loaded into pickup trucks driven by the transportation committee.

The work pits were the pits to clean. But Sabrina pointed out how they could be used for graves, with moldering corpses rising from the dead. That made everyone want to work in the greasy pits.

By dinnertime they had cleaned two-thirds of the factory, and Mr. Kraft showed up with donated pizza and soda for everyone. He and Harvey unloaded a large trunk from his van and placed it carefully in a clean corner of the factory.

"That's our first piece of donated equipment," said Mr. Kraft proudly, as the students gathered around. He opened up the trunk, and he and Harvey took out what looked like a canister-style vacuum cleaner attached to a large fan.

Mr. Kraft smiled boyishly. "It's a fog machine, which the fire department uses for training exercises. It uses a solution that's similar to mineral oil. The fire marshal loaned it to us on the condition that we have clearly marked exits, smoke alarms, fire extinguishers, and flashlights. We want a safe experience for our audience—after we separate them from their money."

"Way cool!" exclaimed Harvey, bending over the strange apparatus. Other students crowded around, poking and prodding it.

Sabrina breathed a sigh of relief, not for the fog machine but for Mr. Kraft's enthusiasm. They had to get the vice-principal on board, too. The fog machine was cool enough to appeal to the little boy in him.

While the kids hungrily munched their pizza, Mrs. Quick assigned some of them to other jobs. The cheerleaders, including Libby and Valerie, were assigned to props and costumes. Their job was to haunt thrift shops, junk stores, and flea markets looking for stuff to use in the scenes.

Old clothes, chandeliers, beat-up furniture, ugly paintings, moose heads—anything that was old and spooky would work. They were supposed to see if they could borrow or rent the props instead of buying them.

Mrs. Quick had worked out a deal with the lumberyard. Tomorrow the transportation committee could pick up some donated plywood, drywall, canvas, paint, nails, and screws. In exchange, the lumberyard would get mentioned in all the ads and flyers. Everybody was supposed to scrounge tools, as they had with the brooms and shovels.

Students who had worked in restaurants were put on the concession committee. Within a few minutes they came up with a ton of ideas for stuff they could sell—from hot dogs and candied apples to glow sticks and balloons.

"We'll make them walk past the concession stand to get in," suggested Mr. Kraft. "That way they'll *have* to buy stuff."

Mrs. Quick formed a budget committee to keep track of expenses, donations, and profits. Before the evening was over, everyone had at least one job, and most of them had more than one. All of them were still on the cleaning committee, too, and they would keep working until the factory was neat and tidy. Then they would get it all dirty and spooky again.

By nine o'clock the cavernous factory was mostly clean, although some dust was still settling. Mrs. Quick decided they could finish up the next day after school. She thanked them all, and they picked up their brooms and shovels and headed wearily to their car pools. Mr. Kraft took a bunch of students who didn't have rides in his car.

Mrs. Quick and Charlie Haynes were somewhere in the back, making sure that her new keys would fit all the locks. One by one the ceiling lights winked off, leaving Sabrina and Harvey alone in a pool of lantern light. It was the first time all day they had been alone together.

He put his arms around her waist and smiled. "You've got to be proud, Sabrina."

"That I have you for a boyfriend?" she asked playfully, putting her hands on his shoulders. "I am."

Harvey looked serious. "No, I mean that you got everyone behind you on this haunted house project. If it wasn't for you, Sabrina, the whole school year would be a bummer. You're the hero of the school."

"Only if we pull it off and make some money," she answered worriedly. "We've got a lot to do before we can congratulate ourselves. We've got to build the maze, rehearse the scenes, publicize it, collect all the costumes and props—"

"You worry too much," said Harvey a moment before he kissed her. Sabrina stopped talking and forgot all about her worries as she melted into his arms.

Mmmm, it was good to be the hero of the school.

* * *

Sabrina was still smiling dreamily when she walked into her house, thinking about Harvey's kiss. He had been so sweet when he drove her home, she could hardly believe it. In fact, everybody at school was being super-nice to her, even people who hated her, like Libby and Mr. Kraft. If she had known it was going to be this easy, she would have been running the school years ago!

The moment Sabrina reached the living room, her good mood was dashed. There sat Aunt Hilda and Aunt Zelda, looking as gloomy as she had ever seen them. They looked as if they had lost their last spell.

"What's the matter?" she asked.

"For one thing, you're home awfully late," snapped Aunt Hilda. She jumped to her feet and began to pace.

"I told you I would be working on the haunted house," answered the teenager. "It's going really well . . . I mean, until now."

"Don't worry about Hilda," said Aunt Zelda. "She's upset about Salem."

"What happened to Salem?" asked Sabrina with alarm.

"He ran away from home."

"Huh? Ran away where?"

Hilda grabbed a neatly printed memo from the coffee table. "He left us this note."

Sabrina took the sheet of paper and read aloud, " 'Dear family, I am sorry to say that I can't live in your household anymore. It's clear that you like the hobgoblin better than you like me, and I really can't blame you.

" 'One of you accidentally left the closet door open, so I'm running away into the Other Realm. Don't try to find me—I won't come back. Thanks for everything. Good-bye. Salem.' " It was signed with a flowing scrawl.

Sabrina frowned. "That doesn't sound like Salem. Are you sure that's his handwriting? Er, pawwriting."

"Who knows?" Hilda asked with a shrug. "I've tried to summon him back with magic, but I can do that only when he's in this realm. If he escaped into the Other Realm, he could be anywhere!"

Her happy mood gone, Sabrina sank onto the couch. "I knew he was upset with all the attention we've been lavishing on the hobgoblin, but I didn't think he would do *this*. Are there any clues to where he went?"

"No," Hilda muttered. "It's all our fault, for not getting rid of the hobby."

"The hobby!" exclaimed Sabrina, leaping to her feet. "He'll do anything, and this is something that needs to be done!"

Sabrina wandered around the room, gazing at the ceiling and hoping the hobgoblin was listening. "Mr. Hobgoblin, could you please track Salem down for us? We're very thankful for everything you've done for us, but we need to have Salem here, too. It's hard to explain why we love him, but he's part of the family."

Zelda dabbed her eyes with a handkerchief. "That was quite moving, Sabrina. Do you think the hobby will find him?"

"Oh, sure! Salem will be back by morning."

"Meanwhile, we can look for him too," said Aunt Hilda, heading for the stairs.

"Let's go!" echoed Sabrina.

"Not you," said Aunt Zelda. "I'll bet you have homework to do."

"Yes, but I could leave it for the—"

"No, you don't," said Zelda, steering Sabrina toward a table. "Do your homework. It's like studying for your witch's license—you won't learn anything unless you do the work yourself. Go on, now."

With resignation, Sabrina stacked up her textbooks on the table. "Okay. But first, what do we have to eat?"

Zelda frowned, puzzled. "It's odd, but a lot of our staples—noodles, beans, and stuff—are missing. Oh, well, I'm sure you'll whip up something." She swept up the stairs.

"Aunt Zelda!" called Sabrina worriedly. "Make sure you find Salem."

"We will," said her aunt with a smile. "As you say, the hobgoblin is probably looking for him, too."

"Help!" screamed Salem as he dangled in a burlap bag hanging from a rope. It was dark inside the bag, and he didn't know where he was, except that it was cold and he could hear rushing water below him.

The cat wanted badly to tear his way out of that bag, but the burlap wasn't very strong. He was worried that if he started tearing at it with his claws, the bag would fall to pieces. That's why he was smarter than the average cat. On the other hand, he couldn't stay hanging in this bag all day, or for the rest of his life. Eventually he would have to try to get out.

That darn hobgoblin! Salem hadn't seen the invisible hands that grabbed him, stuck him in the bag, and whisked him away, but he knew who it was. Just because he had made a little mess in the house. The hobgoblin ought to thank him for providing such a great opportunity to sharpen his cleaning skills.

Maybe the hobgoblin was still hanging around, thought Salem. Maybe he could reason with him.

"Okay, Hobgoblin," Salem said in his most pleasant voice. "You've had your little joke." The cat forced a laugh. "Very funny—I enjoyed it myself. How about letting me out now?"

Nothing happened, except that he was a little colder and felt himself swaying farther, as if the wind had picked up. "Please!" he begged, whimpering. "I want to go home! I promise I'll never make a mess again. I won't even kick the sand out of the litter box! Please get me down from here!"

The cat waited, hoping for some kind of response, but nothing happened. He was still balled up in a burlap bag, swinging from a rope. For several minutes he yowled and meowed, begging to be set free, but the hobgoblin was either deaf or gone. After a while, Salem realized that his enemy was not going to save him.

Then he got angry.

"Okay, Hobgoblin, you've got the upper hand. I may just be a talking cat now, but I was once like you—full of power and meanness. I *still* know how to be mean. You think you're so hot, but you won't come between me and Sabrina. A girl's best friend is her cat. And a witch's best friend is her familiar, not her hobgoblin."

Still no answer, just the gentle sound of rushing water. Salem took a deep breath and realized that he would have to get himself out of this mess. He sprung his claws open and poked them gingerly into the burlap. As expected, the rotten material tore easily. He could rip open the bag in a few seconds, but he didn't know where he was, or what was below him.

The first thing he had to do, thought Salem, was to make a window and see what was going on. Very carefully he tore a three-inch-long gash in the cloth. Then he did it two more times until he had made a crude triangular hole. Unfortunately, the bag was so rotten that every time he moved, it ripped a little on its own. If he wasn't careful, he would fall right out the bottom.

Shifting slowly inside the bag, Salem craned his neck to look out the opening. Gazing straight ahead, he saw a wall of brown rocks some distance away. That meant he was outside, which he had already guessed. Shifting again, he peered upward and could see several steel girders and wooden planks. Hmmm, what did that mean? Whatever was up there, the rope must be tied to it.

Standing on tiptoe and arching his back, the cat managed to peer downward. "Oh, no!" he shrieked. Far, far below him was a raging river full of white rapids! Now he understood his plight: he was in a bag that was hanging from the middle of a bridge over a vast canyon! Below him a rampaging river cut through the wilderness. If the fall didn't kill him, he would drown in the rapids!

The bag began to rip open, and Salem swiftly curled up into a ball. *Maybe if I remain perfectly still,* he told himself, *I can stay alive for a few more seconds.*

But he had weakened the bag by tearing a hole in it, and now it was coming apart at both the top and the bottom. He had to get out, but he was afraid to move! Boy, that hobgoblin was not just mean—he was fiendishly evil! Salem had more respect for the hobgoblin now, but he didn't think he would live long enough to tell him so.

"Okay, Hobgoblin," he croaked nervously.

"The fun and games are over, aren't they? You made your point! Isn't it time to end this silliness and go home?"

The only answer was another ripping sound, this time even louder than before. Salem felt one of his feet poke a hole through the bottom of the bag, and he saw it unraveling at the top. Sunlight came pouring through the ragged material, and the wind chilled him. Desperately Salem reached up and grabbed the rope just as his feet ripped all the way through the bottom. The bag drapped itself around his neck, flapping in the breeze.

"Help!" screamed Salem, swaying back and forth at the end of the rope. He tried to scramble upward, but a cat's claws are designed for digging in, not hanging on. No matter how hard he struggled, he kept slipping off. In another few seconds he would plunge into that cold, rushing water, and he could do nothing to save himself!

It's been a good life, thought Salem, *except that I was never quite able to take over the world.*

With a whimper, the poor cat slipped off the end of the rope and plunged downward—toward the bottom of the canyon. The burlap bag fluttered behind him like a cape, only he wasn't Superkitty. He was falling, not flying.

"Good-bye, cruel world!" he yelled.

Chapter 5

I always wanted to skydive, thought Salem, *but with a parachute!*

As the cat plummeted downward toward the raging rapids far below, he wondered if this was like bungee jumping . . . without the bungee. Salem twisted around in midair, figuring he would land on his feet. Of course, that meant only that he might live for a few seconds before he drowned.

"I'd give anything for a flying vacuum cleaner!" he moaned. "Or even an old broomstick."

The ground and the river were getting closer every second—it was like one of those old cartoons with the stupid coyote. Salem tried to decide whether he wanted to have his eyes open or closed when he died. Closed, he finally decided. Nobody should have to witness his own death.

He scrunched his eyes shut, expecting to hit something hard. Instead he hit something soft. It wasn't water, he decided, because he wasn't wet. And it wasn't the ground, because he wasn't dead. So far, so good.

Very cautiously, Salem opened his eyes. To his surprise, the cat discovered that he was flying through the canyon. *I can fly!* he thought happily. No, that wasn't possible. When he thought about it, he decided he was being carried by an invisible creature who could fly.

"Oh, thank you! Thank you!" he gushed. "I always said you were my favorite hobgoblin."

"Oh, shut up," growled a deep voice. "This sure wasn't *my* idea."

"Well, now that we're friends, can't we work out our differences?" asked Salem. "If we stick together, we could hold out for the really expensive cat food."

Suddenly the invisible hands let go, and Salem was falling again. The bottom of the canyon loomed ever closer.

"Okay, okay!" shouted Salem. "I'll shut up!"

Roughly, he was caught again—this time by the scruff of the neck. Salem was very uncomfortable dangling in the air by his neck, but he didn't say anything.

There will be time enough later to get revenge on the hobgoblin, thought Salem. *Only this time*

I'll be smart—I'll make it look as if the witches want to get rid of him.

Sabrina was sitting on her bed, reading her schoolbooks, when Salem dashed into her bedroom and scurried under her bed. Angrily the teenager jumped off her bed and said sternly, "Salem, come out here! You've been a very bad kitty."

The cat stuck his head out from under the bedspread and looked around furtively. "We can't talk here. Let's go outside."

"Why can't we talk here?" demanded Sabrina. "What's the matter with you, running away like that? You could have gotten hurt."

"No kidding!"

Sabrina walked to her bedroom door and gazed into the hallway. The closet door was still shut, and her aunts were nowhere to be seen. So they must still be looking for Salem in the Other Realm.

"Did the hobgoblin bring you back?" she asked.

"Yes, but . . ." Salem looked around nervously, as if he was afraid to say anything else.

"Thanks, Hobgoblin!" said Sabrina loudly. "What would we do without you?"

"Get a good night's sleep," muttered Salem.

Sabrina put her hands on her hips and glared at her cat.

"What? Isn't it enough punishment that I got turned into a cat? Now I have to put up with a psycho hobgoblin?" Salem lowered his voice. "We've got to talk, but not here."

"No," she said sternly. "I've got to do my homework, and you've got to apologize to my aunts and me for giving us such a scare."

"I gave *you* a scare?" Salem asked incredulously. "Oh, this is hopeless. If you need me, I'll be in my new dungeon under the house." He dashed out from under the bed and scurried down the stairs.

Puzzled, Sabrina shook her head. She knew that Salem was having a hard time adjusting to the presence of the hobgoblin, but this was ridiculous! That cat had to grow up and realize that the world didn't revolve around him.

She went to the nightstand and rubbed her crystal ball. Weird shapes and lights sparkled inside the magical crystal. "Aunt Hilda and Aunt Zelda, this is Sabrina. Thanks to the hobgoblin, Salem is back safe and sound. You can come home now."

Immediately she heard the closet door open, then slam shut. Hilda and Zelda strode into her bedroom, both of them looking very angry.

"Where is he?" demanded Zelda.

"Hiding under the house."

"What is the matter with that cat?" asked Hilda.

Sabrina shrugged. "I don't know. He wouldn't talk to me. If it hadn't been for the hobgoblin, he would still be hiding from us in the Other Realm."

"Salem is just going to have to adjust to our houseguest," said Hilda, "because we like having a hobgoblin. I'd thank him out loud, but I don't want him to leave."

"Salem must be feeling really neglected," said Zelda with concern. "Maybe we should take him to a pet psychologist."

Sabrina frowned. "Won't the psychologist be alarmed when Salem starts talking?"

"A pet psychologist in the mortal realm would be," answered Zelda, "but I know a good one in the Other Realm. He specializes in familiars. I'll make an appointment for Salem." She hurried out of the room.

Hilda scowled. "That cat is so thickheaded and selfish that a psychologist will never do any good."

"We've got to try something," Sabrina said worriedly. "Salem must be pretty desperate, if he tried to run away."

"You mean pretty stupid, don't you?" asked Hilda. "Oh, well, he's safe now—thanks to the hobgoblin."

"Don't thank him too much," Sabrina whispered, "or he'll leave."

"Right. Let's see if Zelda has made an appointment for that crazy cat."

Sabrina followed her aunt out of the room, and

neither one of them heard a low voice whisper, "You're welcome."

When Sabrina woke up in the morning, she listened to the radio while she got dressed. For some reason, morning deejays always felt the need to talk instead of play music, as if stupid jokes and pranks would wake people up.

Sabrina was about to change the station when the cheerful deejay said, "Here's a community announcement about Westbridge High School. The Drama Club and the Pep Club are putting on a Halloween event to raise money. The Halloween Machine is the scariest attraction ever to come to Westbridge, and you can see it only at the old baby-carriage factory at 2300 South Peck Road. The Halloween Machine will be open every weekend, starting on October fifteenth. Admission is only five dollars!"

The deejay chuckled. "We're going to be there to cover the opening night. It promises to be really scary! We'll be giving away free tickets to the Halloween Machine to the next two callers. So pick up those phones and call!"

Sabrina picked up her phone, but it was with trepidation. She hoped it was Valerie and not the hobgoblin who had put that announcement on the air. Sabrina dialed Valerie's number and tapped her foot nervously as the phone rang, hoping her bud would answer instead of her parents. Not everyone appreciated being called at seven o'clock in the morning.

"Hello," came a sleepy voice. Thankfully, it was the right voice.

"Valerie, it's me! I just heard that cool announcement on the radio. Good job! That was your idea, wasn't it?"

"Of course it was," answered Valerie with a yawn. "I put out the press release yesterday. So they're already running the announcement? Great!"

"You're doing a fantastic job," said Sabrina with all sincerity.

"Say, I need your approval for something. I'm designing a flyer on my computer, and I wondered if I should put in a coupon for one dollar off admission. I know lots of people who would gladly pay four dollars in order to save one dollar."

"Me too!" answered Sabrina with a laugh. "My aunt Zelda, for instance. Do it, I approve."

"Thanks, boss."

"Gotta go. See you later." Sabrina hung up with a huge smile on big face. Everything was going to turn out just super!

The next meeting of the Halloween Machine committee was held in Mrs. Quick's classroom after school. It was standing room only. Several kids had heard the announcement on the radio, and they congratulated Valerie for her prompt work. She beamed as she accepted the compliments, and Sabrina grinned right along with her.

"Okay, people, it's time to plan the maze and the scenes we'll have." Mrs. Quick erased the blackboard, then picked up a piece of chalk and drew a big square to represent the factory floor. The teacher carefully marked the work pits, the kilns, and the four exits: the three main doors and the smaller door in the back.

"This is what we have to work with," said Mrs. Quick. "We can put some of the lights, sound equipment, and special effects on the catwalks, and some actors can hide up there. But no customers will be allowed on the catwalks. The fire marshal says we need to clearly mark all the exits with lighted signs."

Mrs. Quick consulted her notebook, then started to draw, slicing up the factory into twisting corridors with sharp turns. "The maze has to be designed so the customers can see only one room at a time, the room they're in. We don't want them to see what's ahead."

Sabrina and the other kids watched in amazement as the crude square on the blackboard was turned into a magical fun house with eight spooky rooms. Mrs. Quick carefully explained how every twist and turn was designed to keep the rooms ahead a secret.

"We should put the elaborate scenes—like Dr. Frankenstein's laboratory—up front. As the customers pass through the maze, we want to scare them and keep scaring them until they flee out the exit, screaming!"

Harvey and the others snickered appreciatively at this plan. There was nothing boys liked to do more, thought Sabrina, than make people scream.

"We'll build ramps and handrails to keep people moving, and to keep them away from the actors and props. If we put the smoke machine on the cat-walk, we can use plastic pipes to pump smoke into three different areas. We'll use the school's theatrical lights and rent strobe lights. Hubert, you were going to look into sound and music for us, yes?"

"Yes," said the student, sitting up straight. "I could only borrow one amplifier, but I have two tape recorders. We can play different sound tracks on seperate channels, so we can have eerie music in the front and screaming in the back."

"Excellent!" exclaimed Mrs. Quick. "Now we just have to figure out what monsters and scenes we want. Any ideas?"

Everyone's hand shot up, and Mrs. Quick fielded their suggestions. Frankenstein and his monster were a popular duo, and everyone wanted to see them. There had to be coffins full of vampires and ghouls, so they decided to use the work pits as a graveyard.

Of course they had to have a torture chamber with various gruesome body parts lying around. The set would be a dungeon, complete with prisoners. They decided to have an alien autopsy room, where the space aliens came back to life and chased the scientists . . . and the customers.

"We'll have to get some lab coats," said Libby, jotting down a note to herself.

They decided not to have any mummies because they moved too slowly, and applying the bandages was a lot of work. But zombies were always cool, and they would have a spooky graveyard in which to lurch around. The last two rooms would be pure Monster Mash, where various monsters would jump out of hiding places and chase the customers out the exit, screaming.

"We can't afford fancy animatronics," said Mrs. Quick. "You know, mechanical figures that move all by themselves. But we can have a few stuffed monsters on springs, jumping out of barrels. And we can fly skeletons and bats down from the catwalk."

The teacher smiled. "The one thing we do have plenty of is *actors*. All of you who don't have a technical job and who aren't working in the concession—prepare to be *monsters!*"

Everyone grinned and applauded. Who could resist the chance to be a horrible monster, frightening people on Halloween?

"I'll draw up the final plans, and Mr. Kraft can take them to the permit office," promised Mrs. Quick. "The rest of you have work to do at the factory. Libby, you're doing great on props and costumes. Valerie, a wonderful job with the press release and media attention, but we need to pass out those flyers."

"I can help with that," offered Sabrina, knowing the job would go faster with witchcraft.

"All right. Move out!" ordered Mrs. Quick.

Salem crouched by a thick cement wall, swishing his tail back and forth as he studied the latch on the gate. The wall surrounded a large yard and an old house a few doors from the Spellman residence. He knew there were two big, loud-mouthed dogs in that yard; he had often driven them crazy by walking on top of their wall. Of course, it wasn't very hard to drive a dog crazy.

He used to torment these dogs just for fun; now he was about to put them to work. He knew every dog in the neighborhood, and they would all help him in his diabolical plan. Dogs were a lot like the hobgoblin, he thought—they would do any stupid thing.

The cat was still angry because the witches intended to send him to a pet psychologist. Well, he would show *them!* Not only was he sane, but he was smarter than any stupid hobgoblin! And it was always better to be smart than sane.

The cat went back on the lookout. After determining that the gate was latched but not locked, he scurried along the wall to the garbage cans in back of the house. He leaped onto one of the lids, which put him close to the top of the wall. With another leap, he was atop the wall.

At once, the two German shepherds appeared below him and began to jump around in circles and bark themselves hoarse. Salem strutted proudly along the top of the wall, causing the dogs to go ballistic. *Ah, is anything more fun than tormenting dogs?* thought the cat.

He noted with satisfaction that a window on the second floor of the house was open. The owners weren't home—they never were at this time of day. So Salem leaped onto the bough of a tree and climbed from limb to limb, making his way toward the window. Of course, seeing this brazen cat in their backyard made the dogs even crazier. They whirled in circles, barking insanely.

"Oh, get a life," muttered the cat. With one more leap he made it to the window ledge. A second later he was inside the house. The dogs could be heard having fits below.

It was a pleasant bedroom, with a telephone on the nightstand. Unlike most cats, Salem had considerable experience making telephone calls, a skill that often came in handy. He pushed the handset off the cradle and listened for the dial tone. Then, with his paw, the cat dialed the number of the Spellman house a few doors away.

He knew quite well that no one was home. But the answering machine was turned on, and that nosy hobgoblin was bound to be listening. The dogs barking in the background would make the prank seem even more real.

"At the tone, please leave your message," said Sabrina's cheerful voice. A beep sounded.

Salem held his nose, trying to disguise his voice. "Hello, Spellman family. This is Arnold Rootmeyer from the Canine Kennels. I have great news for you—those dogs you ordered are here! I know you wanted your new pets as soon as possible, so I'll bring them right over. We don't usually give this many dogs to one family, but we know you'll take good care of them. Your sweet puppies are on their way!"

The cat hung up, chuckling to himself. He dashed across the bed, leaped out the window, and scurried across the tree limbs. The dogs spotted him right away and started barking and jumping around as if they were on pogo sticks.

"Hey, you mangy mutts, follow me! We're breaking out of this joint!" Salem jumped onto the wall and ran toward the gate, with the dogs chasing after him, yapping insanely.

From the top of the gate, he easily popped open the latch. As the gate creaked open, the dogs stopped barking and looked with surprise at the sidewalk and freedom, knowing they weren't suppose to leave the yard.

"Dogs will never rule the world," taunted Salem. "No guts and no brains!" He jumped onto the sidewalk right in front of them and took off.

No dog could resist a cat on the loose; the German shepherds forgot all about the rules as they charged after the fleeing cat.

This was the only dangerous part of Salem's plan, when the dogs were chasing him through the streets. But he knew his route, and he had all his movements planned out. Anyway, he could jump onto trees, cars, and fences, avoiding the dogs, who were stuck on the ground. *Pathetic fools,* thought the cat.

His next stop was the Peterson house across the street, where there was a fat, slobbery bulldog who thought he was bad. He would be plenty bad if he got loose in the living room of the Spellman house with all of Hilda's so-called artwork. Salem snorted with laughter as he led the German shepherds a merry chase.

As he expected, their barking got the fat bulldog all worked up, and he was soon smashing into his fence, trying to reach the animals running wild. Since his gate was usually locked, Salem slithered through a narrow crack in the Petersons' garage door, leaving the frantic shepherds behind him, barking and yowling.

He knew the bulldog had the run of the place and could go in and out of the house through various doggy doors, and Salem figured there was one in the garage.

Once inside, Salem leaped onto the automatic garage-door opener and yanked on the cord with his claw. At once, the door rose majestically, just as the bulldog came tearing through the dog door into the garage. He was so stupid that he couldn't find Salem at first, so the black cat arched his back and hissed loudly. Such behavior was rather melodramatic and uncouth, but it drove dogs wild.

Salem bounded out of the garage and into the bushes. Once again the chase was on!

With a pack of snarling dogs on his tail, Salem dashed to the Dumpster behind the corner grocery store. A couple of grungy stray dogs usually hung out at the Dumpster, and they would be perfect foils for his plan.

Sure enough, near the alley he spotted a scruffy Doberman and a mixed breed who looked to be half pit bull. When Salem shot past them with the other dogs in pursuit, the strays didn't need any encouragment to join the chase. Soon Salem led a pack of five snarling dogs down the street, leaping from car roof to tree to fence.

He had several brushes with death when he barely escaped the snapping jaws, but somehow Salem stayed ahead of the dogs. He was beginning to feel tired and out of breath, and he hoped the result would be worth all this effort. Of course, it was always worth while to make dogs look stupid.

Finally his destination was in sight—the quaint Spellman house, sitting in its perfect yard. Soon it wouldn't be perfect or quaint—it would be a shambles!

Salem had left a small chip of wood in the jamb of the back door, so that when Hilda, Zelda, and Sabrina left, they would think they had shut the door. But they hadn't. As the five hairy, moronic brutes bore down on him, Salem hoped the door was still open. If it wasn't, he would be doggy dinner!

With great relief, he shot through the door and into the kitchen, with the howling pack charging after him. Salem bounded onto the counter, then on top of the refrigerator, while the dogs skidded to a stop and piled into each other. During the confusion, the cat dashed back out the door and pushed it shut behind him. Now the maddened dogs were trapped inside the house, looking for a cat.

Salem jumped to the window ledge and watched the mayhem with amusement. The dogs went tearing around, ripping open the garbage, digging into the cupboards, and eating everything in sight. The bulldog found a pot holder and ripped it to shreds. The strays strewed garbage all over the floor and rooted through it, while the German shepherds licked the dishes.

After a while, the dogs got bored with the kitchen and ran into the living room. Salem hurried around the corner of the house to another window, to keep an eye on them. The crazed pack jumped on the couch, knocked over tables and lamps, pulled down the curtains, and played tug-of-war with the cushions. They shredded a throw pillow and shook it until a cloud of feathers billowed into the air.

Oh, this is delicious! thought Salem. *And I can't be blamed for it, at least not directly.*

He banged against the window, just to make sure that all the dogs saw him. This unleashed another round of frenzied barking, leaping, and running in circles. *Silly mutts,* thought Salem. The cat bounded upward onto a tree limb, making sure the dogs saw him. Some of them were so stupid that they charged up the stairs, looking for him.

He heard a terrible thumping, and a whirlwind began to churn in the middle of the living room. Papers, feathers, and trash swirled into a funnel cloud, as if there were a miniature tornado in the room.

Must be the hobgoblin! thought Salem. The dogs cried and howled, and some of them tried to chase the funnel cloud. This was Salem's cue to leave, and he scurried away from the house as quickly as he could.

That was exactly what the hobgoblin deserved, he thought with a chuckle, to clean up after a pack of wild dogs! Salem was still laughing when he found a nice shady bush across the street to hide under. He would never admit it to the witches, but there were times when being a cat was a major blast!

Chapter 6

In the midst of running errands for the haunted house project, Sabrina had to rush home to pick up a list of advertisers. The hobgoblin had put the list together last night, after studying a stack of football programs and yearbooks.

After that, Sabrina had to meet Valerie and Libby at the thrift shop, then go to the factory for cleaning duty. Sometime between chores she had to get on the phone with the advertisers and do some fund-raising for the fund-raiser! Eating, sleeping—these were not on her to-do list.

The teen opened the front door of her house and charged up the stairs, taking little notice of the five dogs who sat at attention in the living room. She stopped for a moment on the stairs and thought about what she had just seen. *Do we have five dogs?*

"No, we don't even have one dog," she answered herself.

Sabrina went back down the stairs and peered cautiously around the corner of the landing. The dogs were all sitting in a line, wearing pretty bows and new collars, and their fur looked coiffed and styled. Upon seeing her, a couple of the dogs whimpered and started to rise, but two invisible hands clapped together. The sound made the frightened dogs sit back down, staring at her with a mixture of fright and helplessness.

Maybe it was the way they had been freshly bathed and outfitted that told Sabrina the hobgoblin was responsible for this. But why would the hobgoblin bring five dogs into the house? Wasn't Salem enough trouble?

Then again, there was always the possibility that her aunts had something to do with five dogs being in the living room. Odd, impulsive behavior was not unknown to her aunts. Sabrina looked around, thinking she would ask Salem what had happened, but then she realized that he would not have remained in a house with five dogs, even if they were extremely well mannered.

"Did I miss something here?" she asked. "Like . . . whose dogs are these?"

Nobody answered. The dogs wore collars, so maybe they also had dog tags and I.D.'s. Sabrina carefully approached them, checking the smallest one first. Some of the dogs were real brutes, but they all looked well behaved, or at least fright-ened into obedience.

She checked the pit bull's collar and found that he didn't have any tags. Next Sabrina checked a collar on one of the German shepherds, and found that he *did* have a dog license and an I.D. tag. When she saw that his owner lived only a few doors down the street, she suddenly recog-nized him.

"Why, Bruno, I've never seen you so clean!"

The dog whimpered and crouched at her feet. She went to the phone and called up the owners, but no one was home. Sabrina was running late and knew she had to get back to her errands, but she didn't want to leave these five mysterious dogs hanging out in her living room. Then again, they weren't doing anything, and the house was immaculate—as usual since the arrival of the hobgoblin.

Her thoughts were interrupted by a sound from upstairs—the closet door opening and shutting. With relief, she heard her aunts' chattering voices as they sauntered down the stairs. A plaintive bark from the bulldog got their attention.

"Good grief!" exclaimed Aunt Hilda when she saw all the dogs. "What is this—the Spellman Kennels?"

Aunt Zelda crossed her arms. "Sabrina, I think you had better explain this."

"*Me?* I don't know what's going on. I just

came home a few minutes ago and found all these dogs hanging out."

"Well, aren't they precious?" cooed Aunt Zelda, the dog lover in the family. She went right up to them.

"Let's put little hats and vests on them, seat them around the table, and make them play poker," suggested Aunt Hilda, the dog hater.

"I think some of them belong to our neighbors," added Sabrina. "That is, according to their dog tags."

"They look so clean, and they smell so nice," said Zelda. Then she straightened up with a puzzled expression. "They look just like Salem after he was given a bath."

Sabrina nodded. "Yes, I think the hobgoblin has been doing his thing. But that doesn't explain how they got here. Or why."

"Maybe there's a note or an explanation," suggested Hilda. She wandered around the room, carefully avoiding the dogs, and her search took her into the kitchen. Sabrina heard her flick on the answering machine.

Salem's voice, slightly disguised, came out of the machine. Sabrina listened in amazement as the cat pretended to be the owner of a kennel who was to deliver some dogs to the Spellmans.

"That stupid cat!" shouted Hilda. "He's behind all this!"

"The hobgoblin thought they were *our* dogs,"

said Zelda. "That's why he took such good care of them."

Without thinking, Sabrina angrily pointed her finger and caused Salem to appear in the living room in a puff of smoke. He took one horrified look at the canines and shot up the stairs. Immediately forgetting all their good behavior, the pack of dogs became cat-seeking missiles. They knocked Aunt Zelda off her feet as they launched themselves up the stairs in pursuit of the black cat.

"You're going to the psychologist right now!" shouted Zelda, shaking her fist at the departed cat.

"Do you know vy you are here?" asked the bearded man with a German accent.

Salem looked around at the pet psychologist's office, with all the diplomas and letters of recommendation hanging on the walls. There was a letter from a talking parrot, thanking the doctor for curing his split personality. Another letter was from a turtle, thanking the doctor for getting him out of his shell.

"No, I don't know why I'm here," answered Salem. "I don't have any problems at all. But I do like your couch." The cat stretched luxuriously on the soft leather sofa.

The psychologist, Dr. Wernweiner, opened Salem's file and began to read. "Hmmm," he said, scratching his beard. "You ver turned into a cat by zee Witches' Council for trying to take over zee world. You haf been reprimanded a dozen times for trying to avoid your punishment. You haf been arrested and charged with more crimes than any other cat on earth. You pick fights with everybody—most recently a hobgoblin."

"What's your point?" Salem asked snidely.

"Obviously you are antisocial and haf a problem accepting reality."

Salem cocked his head. "I'm a talking cat who lives with three witches, and you say I have a problem accepting reality? If I ever see any reality, I'll accept it. Until then, I choose to believe it's just a nasty rumor."

"But zee hobgoblin," said Dr. Wernweiner, referring to Salem's file. "You can't deny zat you feel a certain hostility toward zee hobgoblin."

"Wouldn't you?" asked Salem, sounding indignant at the injustice of it. "What if somebody came between you and your family? What if you were trying hard to be a loyal pet and familiar and this interloper barged into your house and took your place?"

The cat sniffled pathetically. "Can I wash dishes as well as *he* can? No. All I have to clean with is my tongue. Have you ever tried to clean a house with your tongue? He eats my food, sleeps in my bed, curls up by the fire in my spot, and I have to sleep under the house!

"I tried to be gracious. I thought that if he

liked giving a cat a bath, he would *really* like giving five dogs a bath. I know how much he likes to clean house, so I wasn't as neat and fastidious as usual. Really I should sue the hobgoblin for alienation of affection, but I would prefer to let bygones be bygones."

"Zat is a noble sentiment," said the doctor, sounding pleased. "Perhaps ve can make some progress. Vould you agree to accept the hobgoblin?"

"For how long?" muttered Salem.

"Ve start out easy . . . a couple of weeks. You don't pull any tricks. You just leave him alone."

"I don't want any more baths," warned Salem.

"I vill talk with your mistress." Dr. Wernweiner stroked a crystal ball on his desk, and it sparkled brightly. Sabrina's face shimmered inside the crystal.

"Hello, Miss Spellman. I haf your kitty here. Salem agrees to accept the hobgoblin for two veeks. No funny stuff. Is zat okay with you?"

"That would be great!" Sabrina chirped. "That way it won't interfere with the haunted house!"

The pet psychologist looked puzzled for a moment, but he shook it off. "Vatever you say."

He squinted at Salem. "You live in a haunted house?"

"That's right," Salem lied. "Three witches, a hobgoblin . . . and a goldfish who just floats on his back all day. No wonder I'm high-strung!"

The cat began to sob pitifully, and the doctor reached over and comforted him. "Breathe deeply, Salem. Just tell yourself, 'I'm okay.' It's perfectly all right to be a cat. Cats are good."

"Tell that to a mouse," replied Salem.

"Oooh, look at this!" chirped Valerie as she tried on a tight-fitting beaded flapper's hat from the 1920s. She dashed down the aisle of the musty thrift store, looking for a mirror in which to admire it. She finally found one.

Sabrina nodded appreciatively. "It looks hot on you. But we're not looking for hot, are we?"

"Right." Reluctantly, Valerie took off the elegant hat and set it back on a Styrofoam head on a shelf with twenty other old hats and a few scuzzy wigs.

Sabrina picked up a crumpled fedora and held it out for them to see. "Now *this* says 'Freddy Krueger.' "

At another display in the next aisle, Libby fingered a long white lab coat and smelled it suspiciously. "I suppose this is what the well-dressed mad doctor will be wearing."

"Good, they have a lot of lab coats," said Sabrina. "We're going to need at least six or seven."

Libby sniffed. "This should be your job, Sabrina—picking out weird, crummy clothes."

"I trust your taste perfectly," answered Sabrina with a fake smile.

From a rack of men's clothes, Valerie picked up a white Nehru jacket. "Am I getting closer with this? I mean, it could be for some kind of disco ghoul."

"Good," answered Sabrina. "What about this?" From the same rack of clothes she pulled out an old army jacket that was ripped and frayed. "It couldn't cost much."

"It had better cost zero," replied Libby, "because that's our budget." She draped the clothes they wanted over her arm. "For this fund-raiser, we've gone from selling stuff door-to-door to begging door-to-door."

"But it's for a good cause," said Sabrina helpfully.

"Moose head!" Valerie squealed, pointing to a flea-bitten trophy hanging on the wall.

Sabrina gazed at the massive head with its impressive rack of antlers, feeling more than a little sympathy for the beast. *That's how Mr. Kraft will see me if the Halloween Machine loses money.*

"Hideous chandelier," offered Libby, pointing to a clunky wrought-iron Spanish lamp hanging from the ceiling. It was thick with cobwebs, and it looked like something that might have hung in a medieval torture chamber. "This is just like real shopping, only with bad taste and no money."

The teenage witch checked her watch. "I think the costume committee is doing great! Gotta go."

"Did you drop off the flyers?" called Valerie as Sabrina rushed out the door of the thrift shop.

"Yep!" With the help of witchcraft and the hobgoblin, she was getting everything done.

It was after dark by the time Sabrina reached the factory, and she was out of breath from all the running around. The first thing she noticed when she went in was that all the platforms, paths, and sets had been marked off with masking tape. It was like seeing the foundation of a house. There were no walls yet, but Sabrina could imagine them. When it was all done, the maze was going to be fantastic!

People were working in small groups, cleaning, sawing lumber, unloading trucks, and stacking supplies. The factory was beginning to look like a warehouse for a lumberyard. She spotted Mrs. Quick, Harvey, and the caretaker, Charlie Haynes, on one of the catwalks. They were rigging spotlights and running wire.

As she climbed the stairs near the north wall, she heard Mrs. Quick, say, "We've got to make sure all the lights are secure. We don't want them falling on anyone's head."

"Hi, Sabrina," said Harvey, giving her a warm smile. "If you're looking for something to do, we've got a load of drywall coming in."

"Thanks, Harvey, but I've got about fourteen things to do in the next half hour." She turned to

Mrs. Quick and grinned. "I've collected three hundred forty dollars in donations today!"

"Great!" exclaimed the teacher, batting a cobweb out of her hair. "You're a real go-getter, Sabrina."

Sabrina cringed sheepishly. "Only the donors all want us to put up signs carrying their logos."

"We don't want a bunch of signs around," said Mrs. Quick worriedly. "That will spoil the effect."

"We're going to put banners all around the windows to hide the cardboard," said Harvey, pointing upward. "We'll just put the sponsors' names and logos on the banners."

"Excellent!" replied Sabrina, beaming at her clever boyfriend.

Charlie clucked his tongue like a worried hen. "I hope all this stuff stays up."

"Who would knock it down?" asked Harvey.

The old caretaker frowned and looked down at the metal grating of the catwalk. Mrs. Quick immediately scoffed at him. "Don't tell me you're going to warn us about the haunt again."

"He's been good so far," admitted Charlie. "Could be he doesn't mind having company."

"Could be he doesn't exist," said Harvey.

Charlie shrugged. "I guess he's harmless enough. Stuff might disappear, get moved around. Maybe he thinks he's helping out. But the truth is, there's not much been going on here for a lot of years, even since the work moved overseas. The factory closed down, but they kept me on to look after it. Maybe this old place just has a spirit that won't leave."

"That's the unscariest ghost story I ever heard," said Harvey.

Without warning, the spotlight they had just hung slipped from its socket and dropped twenty feet to the floor below them. The monstrous crash caused all activity in the factory to stop. Everyone froze, as they do when a waiter in a restaurant drops a tray of food. Luckily no one had been standing directly beneath the light.

Sabrina gulped nervously. "Well, he probably could be a scary ghost, if he *wanted* to be."

"Who was the last one to touch that light?" demanded Mrs. Quick. "We must be more careful!"

Mrs. Quick, Harvey, and Charlie looked accusingly at one another, and it was clear that all three of them had been fiddling with the light. Apparently nobody had secured it tightly.

"Yep, the haunt must just be my imagination," said Charlie smugly. "I hope you're right."

Chapter 7

There comes a time in every creative project when the initial excitement wears off, and the hard, relentless work begins. For the next couple of weeks, the haunted house took over the lives of a hundred teenagers, making them cancel parties, miss sporting events, and upset their parents.

Several parents drove out to the old factory to see what had suddenly obsessed their children. When they were handed hammers or paintbrushes, they either ran for their cars or pitched in. They usually didn't come out to see the factory a second time, but all of them promised to come back as patrons when it opened.

At first, the factory looked like a scenery workshop, with flats and lumber lying all over the place. Sabrina marveled at the flats. It was amazing how a length of canvas stretched over a wooden frame could be painted to look like a wall. The illusion was almost like witchcraft.

Slowly the maze began to take shape. Flats were cheap to make and looked okay from a distance, but they couldn't serve as real walls that people might bump into. Unlike theatrical sets, the audience got to walk through this one. So all the corridors and ramps were built of eight-foot-tall plywood braced by sturdy two-by-fours.

Handrails, too, were made of two-by-fours. Some walls were made of drywall, which was almost as strong as plywood. But it was easier to punch a hole through drywall—in case a monster wanted to stick his arm out—and the hole could be plastered over for the next night.

Sabrina was so busy that she didn't see the factory every day, so she was impressed whenever she visited. Something new was always going up, and everyone was excited when the speakers worked or when a picture frame fell as planned, revealing a monster behind it. She felt left out of the action sometimes, but she had plenty of duties.

On this particular night, Sabrina stood at the edge of the parking lot of the Westbridge Mall. There must have been five hundred vehicles parked in the lot, and she was waiting until night fell. Her work was best done in the dark, away from prying eyes.

Finally the sun glimmered its last, and stars

began sparkling overhead. It was now October, and the air finally smelled like autumn—crisp and clean with a scent of spruce. Somewhere in the mall, gingerbread cookies were baking.

She hefted her stack of bright orange sheets of paper and marveled at the flyer Valerie had designed. Over the last couple of days, her friend had perfected it. Everyone was delighted with the layout, the information, the coupon—even the plug for the lumberyard.

Sabrina was glad that nobody had asked her how she handed out hundreds of flyers by herself every evening. They were too busy building handrails and painting flats to care. Certainly nobody volunteered to help her stick flyers under hundreds of windshield wipers. That was Sabrina's job.

Content that it was now dark and most of the people were shopping inside the mall, Sabrina strode through the parking lot. As she approached a row of cars, she grabbed a handful of flyers and flung them into the air like confetti. Wiggling her finger, she guided every sheet under the windshield wiper of a parked car.

Sabrina continued to cruise through the parking lot, sprinkling her flyers like a fairy sprinkling dew on the leaves. When she saw a family walking toward her, she stuffed a few windshield wipers by hand. Once the people had passed, she hurled a handful of flyers at the last row of cars.

They zoomed through the air like a squadron of paper airplanes, landing perfectly under the wipers.

After she finished handing out the flyers, Sabrina planned to check on the progress at the factory. Mr. Kraft was worried sick that they wouldn't be done in time, but every time she visited the factory, she was amazed. She wasn't sure if everything would be done by next week, but they had built wondrous things in a short time.

As she strolled down a peaceful suburban street, Sabrina sent a colorful stream of flyers spinning through the air. As if conducting a concert, she wagged her finger back and forth. Each sheet glided across a front yard and tucked itself neatly under a doorknob. People always wondered how flyers got on their doors without them seeing anyone put them there. If they only knew!

In only a few more days the Halloween Machine would be open, thought Sabrina. Students were working night and day to finish the maze in time, and the publicity effort was going full blast. The monsters were in rehearsal. Even the ghost had been quiet after giving them a few mild scares.

What could possibly go wrong?

Salem studied the bag of groceries on the kitchen counter, his long tail swishing back and forth. For two long weeks he had been true to his word—he'd been the best kitty on the face of the earth. Well, if not that good, he had been awfully good for a certain black cat who used to be a warlock.

Everyone in the family had pretty much forgotten the feud he'd had with the hobgoblin—everyone, that is, except Salem. How could he forget when the hobgoblin was still there? That jerk was still doing his obnoxious good deeds, still kissing up to the witches, and still eating Salem's food! The cat had been sleeping under the house for so long that everyone was beginning to think it was normal.

Oh, Salem's in his little cave under the back porch. How cute!

Even the hobgoblin seemed to have forgotten the feud. He didn't give Salem any more baths; maybe bathing those five dogs had cured him of that. But he still had the run of the house, still whipped through dirt like a whirlwind, and still acted as if he owned the place.

To all appearances, Salem had been good for two weeks, but he was silently and secretly plotting and planning. He knew he would have only one more chance to get rid of the hobgoblin, so the effort had to be good. The cat also knew that this time he couldn't afford to get caught. The witches had to appear to be at fault.

Salem decided to hit the hobgoblin where he lived. What was the one thing he valued more than anything else? His precious meals, when he gorged on Salem's cat food.

The cat unsprung his claws and calmly ripped open the paper sack of groceries. He knew there were cans of cat food near the bottom, because they had almost run out. That was happening with alarming frequency now that they had two mouths to feed.

After dragging two cans of cat food out of the bag, Salem rolled them across the countertop. The cans clattered onto the floor, and the cat held his breath. He had actually done that on purpose, to see if the hobgoblin was on duty and would rush to pick them up. Salem had discovered, much to his delight, that the hobgoblin took time off. Early evenings, like this, he was seldom around. Salem guessed that he had to save his strength for the nighttime chores.

Content that his nemesis was not on duty, Salem rolled the cans out the back door, which he had carefully left open using the chip of wood. In the moonlight he guided his two cans, like a sheepdog herding his sheep. Finally he rolled them through a loose board and into the garage.

There Salem had set up a miniature work-bench on which lay an electric can opener that he had fished out of someone's garbage, a welding kit, a huge mound of chili powder, some red pepper flakes, and a small dish of Tabasco sauce. He had been saving up the hot spices for two weeks, stealing them from the cupboard. No one had noticed.

Having planned this for weeks, Salem was methodical in his preparations. Using the can opener, he reverently opened the two cans of food—from the bottom. It took all of the cat's willpower not to eat any of it, but he was on a mission.

Into each can of food he stirred heaping spoonfuls of chili powder and crushed red pepper. The smell of the pungent spices almost made him sneeze. The cat knew that he might have to eat some of this adulterated food—to make it look good. But that was a sacrifice he was willing to make. He would do whatever it took to get rid of the hobgoblin.

After spiking the cat food, Salem put on a welder's mask, fired up the stick, and welded the bottoms back onto the cans. Not many cats knew how to weld, but Salem was not like many other cats. Welding was a skill he had picked up years ago, when he was still a warlock. He liked any activity that involved flames, sparks, and molten metal.

Salem was counting on the fact that people never looked at the bottom of a can. They opened the top, not the bottom.

Content with his handiwork, he rolled his two cans out of the garage, across the porch, and back into the kitchen. The cans were small enough that he could grip them in his mouth and leap onto the kitchen counter. He couldn't put the cans back in the bag, but it was normal for those paper bags to rip a little.

There were about four cans of cat food left in the bag, so it might be a day or two before the hobgoblin got his special meal. But sooner or later, he would be fed red-hot spices. What would he think about the witches then?

Salem chuckled heartily as he slunk out the door to his hiding place under the porch.

Sabrina materialized in a swirl of sparkles, lighting up the dreary alley between the factory and the railroad tracks. She heard loud music thumping from a CD. player, accompanied by hammers rapping at almost the same beat. Light poured from the wide delivery doors in the back where students were unloading pickup trucks.

Inside the building, electric saws were whirring, and pungent paint fumes floated on the dusty air. There was enough sawdust for a year's worth of high school meat loaf. A horrible werewolf with bulging eyes and yellow fangs walked past her, and two girls rounded a corner carrying a coffin.

Over the loudspeaker, Mr. Kraft shouted, "Okay, clear the graveyard! Zombies, we're going to take it from the top. Cue thunder and fog!"

A peal of thunder erupted overhead, and Sabrina jumped. Lights began to strobe in a lightning effect, and smoke spewed from hidden vents. Already on edge and out of breath, she gasped when a hand grabbed her shoulder.

Harvey grinned at her and pulled his hand away. "Sorry, I didn't mean to scare you."

She laughed nervously. "Isn't that the whole idea of this place?"

"I'm glad you're here," said Harvey. "Bill and I have built the coolest effect, and we want to show it off."

Sabrina started to say that she had to find Mrs. Quick, but the excited look in Harvey's eyes told her that she should see his cool effect first. She glanced around the outer room, which was beginning to look like Frankenstein's laboratory. There were walls painted to look like old bricks, an operating table, and lots of weird electrical coils and equipment, all borrowed from the school science department.

Bill walked through the door, pushing Libby ahead of him. "I've found a human guinea pig," he said. "Hi, Sabrina! Are you coming to see it, too?"

Libby crossed her arms impatiently. "I'm pretty busy, guys. Can you make this fast?"

"Sure," answered Harvey. "Right this way."

The girls fell in behind the boys as they led them through the unfinished maze. Work was going on all around them, and Sabrina tried not to gawk at the newest improvements. Maybe they were crazy and didn't know what they were doing, but they were working awfully hard to make this event happen.

Libby rolled her eyes at Sabrina. "How are things in the real world? I don't see anything but smelly old clothes and rotting moose heads. That's my new life."

"Only three more days, and we'll be be open," said Sabrina encouragingly.

Libby cringed. "Then I'll be *wearing* the smelly old clothes."

"I'll be back in a sec," said Bill, dashing off down a dark corridor.

"Right this way," ordered Harvey. He directed them into a room decorated like a funeral parlor, with velvet curtains and weird chandeliers. Several ornate caskets were on display. One of them was open and had a decaying body in it.

"This is our handiwork!" Harvey said proudly, pointing at the fake body. "Take a closer look."

"I can see it fine from here," said Sabrina with disgust.

"Aw, but you have to get closer," insisted Harvey. "We really worked hard on it. Come on."

Sabrina inched closer to the open coffin, and Libby reluctantly followed. At first, Sabrina was afraid that the corpse was a person in a mask who would sit up and try to scare them. As she studied the corpse, she realized that it was mostly plaster and rubber, but it looked good. Libby pressed closer for a better look.

Suddenly the dead man's chest burst open, and a second monster popped out! The girls screamed in terror and jumped backward as the horrid beast reached for them. When he tried to crawl out of the dead man's chest, Libby was halfway out the exit.

Harvey howled with laughter as the monster leaned out of the coffin and ripped off his mask. It was Bill, who slapped his knee and snorted with delight.

"Not bad," said Sabrina, mustering a weak smile. "Not bad at all."

Suddenly Libby stormed back into the funeral parlor, looking really mad. "Hey!" she yelled. "Isn't that one of the sea chests *I* got for us?"

"Yeah," answered Harvey. "It's a cool one, too."

"But how did you make it so that you could jump out of it?" Libby glared at the boys.

"I just cut a hole in the bottom," said Bill. Then it dawned on him. "Uh-oh."

"Yes, you idiot! I borrowed that chest from the thrift shop, and you cut a *hole* in it! How am I supposed to take it back now?"

As Bill recoiled from the wrath of Libby, Harvey grabbed Sabrina's hand and spirited her away into the maze. They ran down one zigzag platform to another, turned a sharp corner, and found themselves alone in a dimly lit room. Harvey stopped to look back and make sure Libby hadn't followed them.

Sabrina laughed and slid easily into his arms. They gazed fondly at each other, ignoring the hammering, yelling, and scraping all around them. She was about to kiss him when she realized that they were in one of her favorite scenes—the alien autopsy room.

"Oh, wow!" she exclaimed, gazing around with delight. Until now she hadn't seen this room in its almost-finished state. On a bank of shelves were eerie fish tanks and jars containing small aliens floating in colored water. They looked disgusting, although Sabrina knew they were just pieces of old baby dolls and rubber snakes.

Another wall was decorated with posters from famous sci-fi movies, but the four operating tables in the center of the room were the major attraction. They would soon have bulbous-headed aliens lying on them, being dissected—and these dead aliens were going to come to life and chase the mad scientists, and the customers, out of the room.

"Are you still scared?" asked Harvey, wrapping his arms around Sabrina.

"Yes," she lied. "You had better hold me even tighter."

Harvey did as he was told. Just as he was about to kiss her, a horrible growling sounded behind them. Sabrina opened her eyes, certain that one of the teenage monsters had spoiled their romantic moment. She hardly ever got to see Harvey anymore, and she was determined to bawl the intruder out.

She turned to see Mr. Kraft, scowling at her. Again he cleared his throat, which was the growling she had heard. "I don't mean to interrupt anything *important,* but I have to speak with you, Miss Chairperson."

Harvey sighed and gave her a sweet smile. "I'll talk to you later. Maybe I can give you a ride home."

"I'd like that," she assured him. She had been using witchcraft to zip around town, and it would feel good to sit in a car. It'd be even better with Harvey beside her.

After Harvey left, Mr. Kraft frowned disapprovingly. "Miss Spellman, this attraction is a Halloween Machine, not a Tunnel of Love."

"You wouldn't like to get my aunt Zelda in here alone . . . in the dark, holding on to you because she's a little frightened? Perhaps my aunt Hilda might come with you on another night. She'll protect *you.*"

Mr. Kraft grinned stupidly and rocked on his feet. "Yes, it would be nice to show your aunts around. On different nights, of course." He suddenly looked embarrassed. "However, that's not what I wanted to talk to you about."

"I'm listening," said Sabrina.

The vice-principal lowered his voice. "We have a lot of borrowed and donated equipment, tools, and props here now, and I don't want anything to happen to them. I know Charlie means well, but he's not really a night watchman. I think we need to post our own guards—all night long."

"I see," answered Sabrina. When she looked around at all that they had built, begged, and borrowed, she realized Mr. Kraft was right. It was foolish to leave all of this stuff unprotected at night, even though Charlie Haynes was in the back office. Still it was awfully spooky in the old factory, and she didn't know who would want to stay all night.

"Are you going to make kids spend the night here?" she asked doubtfully.

"*I'm* certainly not going to stay here," answered Mr. Kraft with a nervous laugh. "Don't worry—I'll let you come in late to school."

Sabrina shook her head doubtfully. "I don't think parents will let their kids stay all night unless there's a teacher present."

Mr. Kraft scowled, knowing she was right. "Those darn parents are such wimps. All right, either Mrs. Quick or I will be here, too. You set up a schedule for the students. You and I will spend Thursday night here, the night before we open."

"It will have to be voluntary," added Sabrina.

"Whatever," grumbled Mr. Kraft. "This fundraiser had better be worth all this time and effort." He stomped off through the alien autopsy room, still shaking his head.

Would it be worth it? wondered Sabrina. She looked around and marveled at everything that had sprung from her crazy idea—a castle, a graveyard, a squadron of monsters learning to lurch and groan. The Halloween Machine had taken over their lives, just as they taken over this factory.

Harvey knew why it was so cool; it wasn't the monsters, sets, and costumes—it was the way they were all pulling together for the same purpose. Whether they made fifteen thousand dollars or fifteen cents, it was worth it to see everyone working together.

Of course, Mr. Kraft didn't see it that way. If they lost money, it would be a disaster, and he would never let her forget it.

Why worry? thought Sabrina decisively. In a few days the Halloween Machine would be open, and they'd be raking in the money! Nothing was going to go wrong.

Chapter 8

On Wednesday the building inspector came out and approved their temporary changes to the old factory. After he left, there was a lot of applause and slaps on the back. They were free to open on Friday, if they finished everything on time.

On Thursday night the paint was still wet, and a crew was still building the concession stand outside, but the maze was finished. From various areas of the maze came loud groans and growls as the teenagers rehearsed their monster roles.

"More groping, more shuffling!" Sabrina directed a troupe of four backup zombies on the cemetery set.

Harvey was one of the undead, and he stopped in midlurch and stared at her. "What's my motivation?"

Sabrina rolled her eyes. *Actors.* "You're hungry, and the customers look like a bunch of cheeseburgers."

Valerie, who was also a backup zombie, looked at Harvey and shrugged. "At least there aren't many lines to remember. Just 'uurrgh' and 'aarrgh.' "

"Okay, zombies, back to your graves!" shouted Sabrina. "From the top. When I give you the cue, pretend that a new group of customers has just entered. Each one looks like a ham sandwich."

She licked her lips and looked at her watch. *I'm hungry too, and once again I'm missing dinner. What we do for love!*

The sound of the can opener caused Salem's ears to perk upward, and his whiskers shot out like radar antennas. A can being opened was always a call to rejoice, even more so lately, as he was waiting for one of his special cans to be opened. He had noticed the way they were stacked in the cupboard, and this could be the moment.

The black cat leaped onto the counter and cautiously approached the can opener, which was under the control of Zelda. Did he get a whiff of chili powder? Zelda shooed him away as she continued talking to Hilda: "So I told him that he couldn't have the name of my accountant, who was working exclusively for me!"

Aunt Hilda chuckled. "Yes, I was wrong about the hobgoblin. I thought he did a good job putting in the new sprinkler system."

Zelda spooned cat food into the hobgoblin's dish. She wasn't paying any attention, so she didn't notice that it smelled like chili and red-hot Tabasco. "I've been thinking of asking the hobgoblin to paint the laundry room," said Zelda. "Do you have any thoughts on the color?"

"How come you haven't played a joke on him yet?" asked Salem. "You're such kidders, you two! You'll have to get him with a real zinger one of these days."

"Oh, Salem," said Hilda with minor irritation. "How about lime green?"

"That sounds good." Still mulling it over, Zelda set the hobgoblin's dish on the floor.

Salem backed toward the open door, his tail twitching nervously. He had always considered cat food awfully bland; anyone who actually liked it couldn't have any stomach for spicy food. They were eating dinner a bit late, and the hobgoblin appeared to be hungry—the cat food disappeared even faster than usual.

The first sign that something was amiss occurred when the pots and pans in one of the lower cupboards suddenly banged together. It sounded as if something large had just been hurled into the cookware.

"Goodness!" exclaimed Zelda, jumping away

from the counter. "What is going on? Is that you, Salem?"

The cat was laughing so hard, his eyes began to tear up. "Don't tell me you did the old Tabasco-in-the-cat-food trick on him! I'll never forget when you did that to me. I couldn't talk for a month."

The aunts glanced at Salem, but their attention was diverted by a plume of water that shot out of the faucet and sprayed the ceiling. The new outdoor sprinklers came on, shooting a stream of water through the window, drenching the two aunts.

The garbage disposal began to growl ominously, as if it were trying to swallow a frying pan. Dishes flew out of the cupboards and soared across the kitchen, aiming right for Hilda and Zelda. Shrieking, they ducked and ran for cover.

From hiding places behind chairs and doors, Hilda and Zelda aimed their fingers at the flying saucers. They zapped several of them into smithereens, but there were just too many plates and cups swirling all at once. It was a blizzard of crockery!

When a plate smashed into the door just above his head, Salem flattened himself on the tile floor. He knew he should run for it, but this was too entertaining. *Who wanted all that neatness and cleanliness? This is what I crave—chaos and rubble!*

Then something amazing happened. Hilda got picked up bodily off the floor. Flailing her arms and legs, she was helpless as some invisible force carried her up the stairs. Salem wasn't sure what happened after that, but he heard the closet door slam shut.

Zelda jumped to her feet and started mumbling, trying to cast a spell. But the hobgoblin was just too fast for her. A whirlwind chased her into the corner and scooped her up. Twisting and kicking, she was carried up the stairs and whisked away.

Maybe the hobgoblin would give them a bath, thought Salem. The cat was amazed. He knew the hobgoblin was bad, but he didn't expect him to dispense with two full-grown witches so easily.

When Salem heard terrible thumping and crashing sounds coming from upstairs, he had to find out what was happening. Charging out the back door, the cat climbed the nearest tree and peered into a second-story window. He saw dressers, beds, tables, and other furniture piled against the closet door.

He figured that Hilda and Zelda had been banished to the Other Realm, and the hobgoblin was going to make sure they stayed there awhile. This wasn't quite what the cat had expected. He thought the household spirit would just get mad and leave, not kick the witches out. *Hmmm,* thought Salem, *too bad I don't have a backup plan.*

The house was eerily quiet, as if the hobgoblin was waiting for something. Or maybe he had left the house. But where would he go? What would he do next?

"Sabrina!" called Mr. Kraft. In the dark maze, she couldn't tell where his voice was coming from, but he sounded altogether too pleasant and cheerful.

The teenage witch was cautious as she rose from the director's chair. "Keep practicing your lurching and growling," she told the actors in the graveyard. "I'll be right back."

"Take your time," answered Harvey.

"Sabrina!" called Mr. Kraft again.

She followed his voice through the maze. When she found him, she realized why he sounded so pleasant—Aunt Zelda was with him. She always brought out the best in Willard Kraft, although no one knew how she did it.

Sabrina was pleased to see her aunt. "So what do you think of this place?" she asked excitedly.

"Pretty amazing," answered Aunt Zelda. "I can see you've done an awful lot of work."

"No kidding," said Mr. Kraft. "There were times when the students wanted to give up, but *I* kept encouraging them. I told them we could do it, despite the odds."

Sabrina tried not to roll her eyes with disgust. "Yes, Mr. Kraft has been a true inspiration."

"I understand the two of you are supposed to spend the night here tonight," said Aunt Zelda.

"We have to protect all this stuff we borrowed," explained Sabrina. "We open tomorrow, you know. The press will be here and everything."

"I know," answered Zelda with an enigmatic smile. "I think you should come home and eat some dinner and take a nap before you stay up all night."

"An excellent idea," said Mr. Kraft. "You run along, Sabrina. I'll work with the zombies. Goodness knows, I get enough experience working with zombies at school."

"Everyone should wrap up early tonight," said Sabrina. "We're all really tired."

"All right, I'll send the students home," agreed the vice-principal. "But I'll see you later, Sabrina. Thanks for coming by, Zelda. Maybe I can give you a private tour of the Halloween Machine."

"I would like that," said Zelda with a soft purr in her voice. "Come along, Sabrina."

After they stepped outside into the cool night air, Sabrina looked curiously at her aunt. There was something odd about her, although she couldn't figure out exactly what it was.

"I don't really need to take a nap," she said. "I can just use a stay-awake spell."

"Let's head home," replied Zelda. "We'll talk about it there." The elegant witch snapped her fingers, and Sabrina found herself standing in her own kitchen. It smelled as if a chocolate cake was baking in the oven and beef stew was simmering in a pot on the stove.

"Oh, man, I am so hungry!" said Sabrina, checking out the food. "Thanks for coming to get me."

"No problem," answered Zelda. "You go ahead and eat. I have to check on something upstairs."

"Great!" Hungrily, Sabrina dished up a steaming bowl of beef stew. She sat down at the kitchen table and dug into the food, savoring every delicious mouthful. After a few minutes, she began to feel so incredibly sleepy that she could barely keep her eyes open.

"Maybe I do need a nap," she murmured with a yawn. She stood up, feeling wobbly on her feet. A desperate scratching sound came from the back door, but she ignored it. After all, it was probably just Salem, begging for leftovers.

Until that moment, Sabrina didn't realize how tired she was from all the late nights and hard work. She staggered into the living room and slumped onto the couch. As soon as she stretched out, she was asleep. In blissful oblivion, the teenager snored peacefully.

She didn't hear a diabolical chuckle coming

from the top of the stairs. "Feed *me* chili powder, will you?"

The chime of the doorbell finally woke her up. Sabrina bolted upright on the couch, barely remembering how she had gotten there. She looked at her watch and saw that it was eleven o'clock. *I have to get back to the haunted house,* she reminded herself.

But first I have to answer the door. Wearily she shuffled to the door and opened it. Her bleary expression was instantly replaced by one of delight, because there was Harvey, standing before her in all his charming splendor.

He gave her a sheepish smile. "Can I come in?"

"Sure!" Sabrina motioned him into the house. "You're just in time to give me a ride back to the factory."

As Sabrina looked for her jacket, she rubbed her eyes. "Boy, I was really tired. I lay down for what I thought would be just a second, but I would have slept all night if you hadn't come."

His expression grew unexpectedly grave. "I have something important to talk to you about, Sabrina."

"Don't worry about the haunted house," Sabrina assured him. "Everything will work out fine."

"It's not the haunted house that's bugging me," said Harvey. "It's us."

"Us?"

"Yes, I don't want to date you anymore," said Harvey bluntly. "I've fallen in love with Libby."

Those two sentences were like two fists hitting Sabrina in the stomach, and she doubled over in emotional pain. "What?" she asked shakily. "I'm still sleeping, right? This is a really bad dream."

"It's no dream," he said matter-of-factly. "Our romance was fun for a while, but I need someone more mature."

"Libby?" Sabrina asked in amazement. Tears began to well up in her eyes. This couldn't be happening, could it?

"But everything has been so great between us!" she protested through her tears. "You've never been more romantic, and you've been telling me what a great job I've been doing!"

Harvey shrugged. "One has nothing to do with the other. The truth is, Sabrina, you're too weird for me. I'll still see you around school, but don't expect me to talk to you. Good-bye, Sabrina."

With that, he strode out the door and slammed it coldly behind him. Sabrina stared pathetically at the place where he had stood, a lump of sorrow in her throat. *My sweet Harvey has just dumped me!* In the past she had given him many excellent reasons to dump her, but he had always stayed true. Now, when things were going great, he was gone!

Sabrina fell back onto the couch, buried her face in her hands, and cried.

When Mr. Kraft heard an ominous thud coming from the back of the factory, he gritted his teeth and tried to ignore it. Mrs. Quick and the caretaker had warned him that the factory was full of strange sounds—things that went bump in the night. But there was a lot of old wood and new construction, which had to settle. At least that's what the vice-principal kept telling himself.

"Where is that darn Sabrina?" he grumbled. "She should've been here by now. She's never punctual!"

He busied himself painting handrails for a while. Then he inspected the two strobe lights they had rented from a theatrical supply house. Around Halloween, strobe lights were in big demand, so they couldn't get them free. Finally Mrs. Quick had bitten the bullet and rented them at full price, holding off delivery as long as possible.

The lights had not arrived until this afternoon, and there hadn't been time to put them in place. The students would hang them tomorrow before the press arrived, but Mr. Kraft wanted to make sure they worked. If they didn't, he would promptly get a refund and save a few dollars!

"Might as well plug them in," said Mr. Kraft.

"I have to do *something* while I wait for Sabrina Spellman to show up."

Mr. Kraft plugged the two strobes into an electrical power strip and lined them up, pointed at the tombstones in the graveyard. Under those tombstones were the work pits, from which gruesome corpses would soon rise. For the first time, Mr. Kraft was actually looking forward to Halloween. The little boy in him wanted to see all the lights, sound effects, actors, and fog in action.

But when he plugged the power strip into the main circuit, all the lights in the factory went off. "What now?" he snapped as he fumbled for the flashlight attached to his belt.

After juggling the flashlight, he finally pointed the beam in the right direction. From a distance, the master light panel appeared to be okay. There was no reason for the room to be plunged into darkness. Unless this was the work of . . . the ghost!

Suddenly a door slammed shut, which made him jump. Had somebody just come in? It was hard to tell where the sound had come from, because they had added interior doors on some of the sets. A monster slamming a door was a cheap and easy scare.

Mr. Kraft listened, and he was certain that he heard footsteps. Or was it more like shuffling sounds? "Charlie?" he croaked. "Is that you?"

At once, the flats and walls were struck by wildly pulsing strobe lights—like an indoor lightning storm! The flashlight was ripped from his hand, and Mr. Kraft shrieked and staggered backward.

He was surrounded by horrendous cracking sounds, as if the walls were being torn apart! A howling wind hit his face, and the strobe lights blinded him. Something whizzed through the air and smashed into the flat behind him, and Kraft heard the ripping of canvas. Terrified by these sounds, he plunged blindly toward the wall, until his feet flew out from under him.

With a scream, Kraft pitched forward into an open grave, crushing a skeleton made from papier-mâché. As he thrashed about among the fake bones, the din grew louder and more ferocious. With sharp explosions, the strobe lights shattered, and once again the factory was plunged into total darkness.

Trembling with fear, Mr. Kraft dug deeper into the grave. *Something* was ripping apart the Halloween Machine, and he just wanted to stay alive!

Chapter 9

Sabrina was so busy sniffling and feeling sorry for herself after Harvey broke up with her that she didn't hear Salem scratching at the door. She didn't pay any attention to him until he began to howl like an alley cat. At first she couldn't believe that *was* Salem, but then she saw a black cat perched in the oak tree, trying to get her attention.

Yowling and flailing his paws desperately, he fell off a branch and crashed to the ground. Sabrina immediately rushed outside into the brisk night air. At first glance, it appeared as if his fall had been broken by a pile of autumn leaves. But the poor kitty wasn't moving!

Sabrina swept Salem up in her arms, and he was as limp as a Beanie Baby. Already emotionally overwrought, she cried even louder as she clutched the injured cat to her chest. "Oh, my poor kitty! What's the matter with you? Did you hurt yourself?"

"No," he answered with a yawn. "I'm just exhausted from trying to get your attention. Don't you ever answer the door anymore?"

"I wish I hadn't answered the door," muttered Sabrina, looking crushed. "Harvey was just here, and he broke up with me."

"I'm not so sure that *was* Harvey."

"What do you mean?" She stared suspiciously at her talking cat.

"It's just a theory. But when Harvey left, he didn't climb into a car—he turned into a meteorite and streaked across the sky, headed downtown."

Sabrina frowned at her familiar and sniffed. "Oh, you're just trying to make me feel better. If that wasn't Harvey, then who was it?"

Salem cocked his head. "A certain hobgoblin who's gone bonkers."

Now she scowled openly at him. "Bad-mouthing the hobgoblin won't help anything."

"Go upstairs and see what he's done to the interdimensional closet," suggested Salem. "And tell me what he's done with your aunts."

Still doubtful but curious, Sabrina returned to the warmth of the house, still carrying her cat. She had been wondering where Aunt Hilda and Aunt Zelda were, especially since Zelda had come home with her. She carried Salem up the stairs and was more than a little surprised to see all the furniture from the bedrooms piled up in front of the closet door.

"Oh, no!" Sabrina set the cat down, then rolled up her sleeves and intoned:

Dresser, nightstand, table, and chair,
What the heck are you doing there?
Get up right now, go with a zoom.
I'm sending you all to your room!

She pointed her finger, and the furniture dematerialized into swirls of crackling, pulsing light. Immediately the closet door flew open, and Hilda and Zelda tumbled out in a heap, as if they had been pushing on the other side. Both of them looked harried, frazzled, and wet.

"Sabrina!" exclaimed Zelda, jumping to her feet. "Are we glad to see you!"

"Didn't I come home with you from the factory?" asked the teenager with confusion.

"No way. We've been trapped in that closet for hours! The hobgoblin must have put a spell on it."

Hilda brushed mud off her dress. "He just went bonkers. I *said* you couldn't trust a hobgoblin. I told you so!"

"So did I," muttered Salem, shaking his head sadly. "But would anybody listen to the voice of wisdom? All you listened to was the siren song of the hobgoblin. They all go bad sooner or later."

Sabrina's jaw dropped open. "He impersonated Harvey, and he impersonated you, Aunt Zelda. Where is he now? What is he doing?"

"He could be up to more mischief," admitted Zelda. "He knows all about our lives ... everything we do, everybody we know."

"Ahem." Salem cleared his throat. "Didn't I say he was headed downtown?"

"The Halloween Machine!" Sabrina went into panic mode. Luckily she was a witch, so panic mode could actually do some good.

"Follow me!" she said as she snapped her fingers. All three witches disappeared in a haze of phosphorescent sparkles.

They reappeared with a dramatic poof in the middle of the parking lot of the old factory. The concession stands were up, which made the parking lot a little more cheerful, but not much. Although it was late at night, Sabrina could hear smashing and crashing sounds coming from the dark brick building. Looking closer, she spotted a figure crawling away from the east door.

Running at full speed, she reached him a second before her aunts. It was the caretaker, Charlie, and he had an ugly bump on his head.

"Charlie, what happened to you?" asked Sabrina.

"He's going crazy in there," muttered the old man. "I never saw him go so wild."

"You know the hobgoblin?" Aunt Hilda asked with surprise.

"Who?" muttered Charlie, holding his fore-head. "I'm talking about the ghost."

"There's a ghost, too?" asked Aunt Zelda.

"Never mind about that," said Sabrina wor-riedly. "We've got to do something!"

Zelda pointed her finger at Charlie and said:

Keep this man safe, and freeze him here,
Until there's nothing left to fear.

A beam of sparkles shot from her finger and enveloped the old man; he froze in place, gaping at them.

"Let's go!" Sabrina jumped to her feet and led the way into the building with her aunts right behind her.

It was very dark inside the old factory, with only a little moonlight spilling through the open doorway and broken windows. When something whizzed past Sabrina's head in the darkness, she saw it just in time to duck.

Behind her, Aunt Hilda caught the chunk of wood in midair. "Let's have a little light in here," she grumbled.

Hilda pointed her finger upward. With an explosion of sparks, the overhead fluorescent bulbs blazed on, illuminating the vast space with bright light.

Sabrina gasped. Half of the maze was a sham-bles. Splintered wood and smashed flats littered the building like the remains of a tornado. The other half of the maze was still intact, and Sabrina could see why. A shimmering wall seemed to protect the undamaged sets from a black funnel cloud of sawdust, dirt, and debris.

The whirlwind kept slamming itself into the shimmering wall, which bulged outward but didn't collapse from the terrible assault. The battle raged all across the factory, from the catwalks to the kilns. Sabrina had never seen anything like it. One mysterious force was protecting the maze from an even weirder force.

But the protector was losing, as more of the flats and walls kept getting chewed up in the momentous battle. If the witches didn't do something quickly, there wouldn't be anything left to save.

"Stand together!" shouted Hilda over the din. "We must hold hands and combine our powers!"

Sabrina did as she was told, trusting her aunts to know what to do in this crisis. She stood between them, and they locked hands. Hilda and Zelda each had a free hand, which they pointed at the rampaging whirlwind, as Hilda intoned:

Hobgoblin, you were good for so long.
Now you've flipped and done us wrong!
At the count of three, you will be gone—
Back to wherever you belong!

* * *

"One!" shouted Zelda.

"Two!" chimed in Sabrina.

"Three!" yelled Hilda.

Bolts of magical energy shot from Hilda's and Zelda's hands, enveloping the black funnel cloud. Under the onslaught, the whirlwind began to shrink, and the shimmering wall drove it back to the wrecked part of the factory. Then the chaos began all over again, as more boards and props flew through the air. The hobgoblin wasn't leaving!

Sabrina could feel herself weakening as the magic drained from her. She could barely stand up, and she would have fallen over if her aunts hadn't been there to hold her up.

Suddenly the black cloud morphed into a human being—Harvey! He stood amid the wreckage, laughing at them. "You fools! I belong with *you*, my masters! You'll never get rid of me that way."

"Oh, darn," muttered Hilda, dropping her hand and letting the spell fizzle out of her fingertips.

"If we're your masters," said Sabrina, "why are you doing this?"

"Because you ticked me off!" The fake Harvey suddenly grew into a giant Harvey, twenty feet tall. He laughed insanely and began to stride through the maze. With huge, thumping footsteps, he kicked and smashed everything in his path.

"I'll take care of him," said a strange voice.

Sabrina looked up to see a fist form out of the swirling dust. It swung through the air in a gigantic arc and smashed into the hobgoblin's face, knocking him backward through a portrait of a vampire. Sabrina flinched, because the hobgoblin still looked like Harvey.

She watched in horror as the invisible Titans grappled in midair and on the floor, crushing sets and props under their magical weight. If this went on much longer, there would be nothing left to save!

Then Sabrina remembered something—the way Aunt Zelda had cautioned her not to thank the hobgoblin too much or he might go away. She had to try it! With the Halloween Machine crumbling all around them, she had no time to explain her plan to her aunts.

"Grab my hands!" she ordered. Zelda and Hilda quickly obeyed, and Sabrina shouted:

Do it, Hobgoblin! Wreck this place!
Send all this junk into outer space.
Smash it all—the sets and planks.
To you, Hobgoblin, we give our thanks!

Not one thank-you, not even two!
No, Hobgoblin, a *billion* thanks to you!
A thank-you for every star in the sky.
Our thanks to you will never die!

* * *

Once again the witches lifted their arms. Only this time pastel rainbows flowed from their fingertips, engulfing the giant Harvey in sweet heart-shaped clouds.

"Oh, rats!" groaned the hobgoblin. With a sigh he began to disappear. "You're welcome!" he muttered.

And then—*poof!* He was gone.

Groaning with relief, Sabrina let go of her aunts' hands. Her palms were clammy and trembling—both of those spells had taken a lot out of her.

Hilda proudly slapped her on the back. "Great job, Sabrina! Next time maybe you'll listen to my warnings about hobgoblins."

Sabrina rolled her eyes. "Excuse me, Aunt Hilda, but the only one who really warned us was Salem. If it hadn't been for him, we would've been too late to save the Halloween Machine."

"We were almost too late anyway," said Aunt Zelda, gesturing around at the wreckage.

Hilda sighed. "We could fix this with witchcraft, but we don't know what it looked like to begin with."

"I do," said a soft voice.

Sabrina looked up to see a slight shimmer on the catwalk above them. It coalasced into a small girl, who smiled mischievously at them, as if she had been playing hide-and-seek.

"You're the haunt," said Sabrina. "Thanks for holding the hobgoblin off until we got here."

"I couldn't let him destroy everything you'd built," answered the odd voice. "But I didn't want to fight a fellow hobgoblin."

"So that's what you are," grumbled Hilda with disapproval.

"Retired." The hobgoblin curtsied. "I thought I was finished with this old factory—that I would never have any chores to do again. The original owner was a warlock, you see. I really just wanted to retire in peace—I never imagined I would have to protect it from a fellow hobby."

Sabrina gave the spirit a sympathetic smile. "I guess it was quiet here, just you and old Charlie."

"Until *you* showed up," hissed the hobby. "I resented you at first, and tried to scare you away. But you were having so much fun! I remembered the old times, when the factory was full of people, and I didn't mind it so much."

A ghostly sigh wafted through a curtain of dust. "Now everyone will think *I* did this."

"If you really know how it all went together," said Hilda, "we can fix it as good as new."

"Oh, I know," said the hobgoblin. "I know every inch of this place, and everything that's in it. Don't worry, I'm an excellent cleaner."

Suddenly a loud groan sounded behind them, and Sabrina whirled around to see a white-faced corpse rising from the grave. His hair was sticking out at odd angles, and he was covered in sawdust and plaster. As he stumbled out of the grave,

Zelda shrieked and aimed her finger to zap the horrid apparition.

"Wait!" whispered the hobgoblin. "He's one of yours."

"He is?" asked Zelda with surprise. She put on her glasses and peered closely at the bedraggled monster. "Willard?"

"Aaargh!" moaned Mr. Kraft, sounding more like a zombie than any of the students who were supposed to play zombies.

Sabrina instantly pointed her finger at him. "Freeze!"

Mr. Kraft froze, looking like the mummy, with his outstretched hand and confused expression.

"One of us has to take him home," said Sabrina, "and tell him . . . something."

Aunt Zelda walked around the frozen vice-principal, inspecting him as if he were a statue. "He obviously hit his head, the poor dear. I doubt if he'll remember much about what happened."

"You take him home," said Hilda. "When Willard is dazed like that, he'll believe almost anything. The hobby and I will get started in here. Sabrina, you should tend to that man in the parking lot."

"Oh, right!" exclaimed the teenager. "What will I tell *him?*"

From the catwalk, a voice whispered, "Tell Charlie that the haunt won't be around anymore. When you thanked your hobby, I also got enough thanks to last me for all my years here. I know it's time to move on, as soon as I help to tidy up the place."

Hilda rolled up her sleeves. "First get the wounded mortals out of here."

As Zelda took charge of Mr. Kraft, Sabrina rushed outside to the parking lot. She found Charlie right where she had left him, on his knees, frozen. "Okay, Charlie, when you unfreeze, you'll think it was no more than a sneeze."

She pointed her finger at the old man, and he fell forward onto his hands. Sabrina steadied him. "Easy there. Just relax."

"But the ghost!" said Charlie, staggering to his feet and adjusting his glasses. "At least . . . I *thought* I saw the ghost."

"No, you sneezed and hit your head," insisted Sabrina. "Don't you remember?"

The old man stared at her and touched a bump on his forehead. "I do kind of remember that. But I thought it was a board that hit my head. Boy, I must have been hallucinating. Maybe I should sleep at home tonight."

"Good idea," agreed Sabrina. "For both of us."

"Are you sure everything is okay with your fun house?"

Sabrina rolled her eyes. "It had better be."

Chapter 10

Under a full moon on a crisp autumn night, four draft horses were pulling a wagon full of hay and people. They weren't going very fast, just a nice trot around the parking lot, but Sabrina could hear the passengers shrieking with delight. The lights of the TV station's camera crew played on the bucolic scene, and Sabrina grinned.

The old factory looked great! As Mrs. Quick had predicted, the gnarled vines seemed almost festive with skeletons and ghosts hanging from them. Banners on the windows, sporting sponsors' names and logos, gave the Halloween Machine a corporate feel. It seemed quite natural to throw your money away here, thought Sabrina.

Judging from the line of customers waiting to get in, plenty of people were willing to do so. Kids had come from all over the county, including some high school students she hardly ever saw. While they waited, they studied the carved pumpkins that lined the walkway, and the pumpkins watched them with jagged, orange eyes. Tiny skeleton lights danced in the breeze.

With the TV crews, concession stands, hayride, and customers, the parking lot was frantic and chaotic. But it was a good chaos, thought Sabrina.

A flashbulb startled her, and she turned to see Valerie and Libby getting their pictures taken with the reporter from the newspaper, Janice Raymond. They were about to take a tour through the haunted house, and Sabrina had just the right crew to accompany them.

From the line she pulled three giggling ten-year-old girls. She knew that nobody could scream like a ten-year-old girl, and she wanted there to be lots of screaming.

"Would you like to get in free?" she asked.

"Sure!" they answered.

Sabrina took the girls to the concession stand, where Valerie was showing off the items they had for sale. "We're offering traditional autumn treats," she began. "Hot apple cider, candied apples, candy corn, and gingerbread cookies."

"Along with sodas, candy bars, and hot dogs," chirped Libby. "For the more plebeian-minded."

"And these special glow sticks," said Valerie, breaking out a box of long, thin plastic tubes.

She looked around, spotted the girls with Sabrina, and handed them the glow sticks. They jumped with delight. Sabrina showed them how to crack the membranes inside the tubes and mix the chemicals, making the sticks glow an eerie phosphorescent green.

Sabrina winked at Valerie and pointed to the girls. Her friend nodded and smiled—they were on the same wavelength, and the girls would go with the reporter. Making her voice as spooky as possible, Valerie intoned, "Now it's time for all of you to enter the Halloween Machine."

The young girls squealed with delight, and so did Janice Raymond. Even her gray-haired photographer looked excited as he followed them down a gauntlet of tombstones and into the entrance to the Halloween Machine.

"I'll take over," Sabrina whispered to Valerie.

"Thanks," said the head of publicity, rushing off to intercept a TV camera crew.

Fog and eerie music greeted their arrival in Frankenstein's laboratory. In the dim light, strings hanging from the ceiling brushed against their faces, causing even the bravest visitors to flinch. To make the effect all the more real, spectacular cobwebs hung from every corner of the laboratory. Weird Tesla coils and electronic equipment pulsed and hummed.

Dr. Frankenstein and his hunchbacked assistant, Igor, frolicked around the monster, who was strapped to a large operating table. Various organs and body parts hung from hooks on the wall, in case they needed a spare part. With dramatic gestures, like actors in a silent movie, Frankenstein and Igor began throwing all the switches on the wall.

When the strobe lights started, so did the screaming.

"It's alive! It's alive!" shouted an eerie voice over the loudspeaker. Silhouetted in the flashing strobes, the hulking monster broke his straps, rolled off the table, and lurched toward the audience. That was all it took to send them fleeing down the narrow corridor to the next exhibit.

The next setting was the funeral parlor, where Harvey had worked so lovingly. Thanks to the twisting maze, the customers were forced to brush against coffins occupied by yucky dessicated bodies. As the visitors stopped to look at one gruesome corpse, Sabrina held her breath. Suddenly a monster popped out of the dead man's chest, groping and growling.

It was a scream fest as the ten-year-olds led the way out, and the photographer squeezed off a couple of nice shots.

Now they were in the graveyard, but that was hardly a better place to be. The Halloween Machine didn't have a lot of special effects, but they had plenty of actors to make up for it. Sabrina had to admit that the fog stealing across the tombstones was pretty impressive, especially when the ghouls, vampires, and zombies began to crawl out of their graves.

Next came a torturous walk through a twisty part of the maze, complete with slamming doors and growling monsters popping out of dark corners. They had stooped to all the usual fun-house tricks—jets of air, swooping bats, and loud, unexpected noises.

Finally the intrepid party reached the torture chamber, complete with a rack, a wheel, a guillotine, and various other torture devices. Chains, fake bodies, and body parts hung from the rafters. When the guillotine suddenly dropped with a loud *ka-chunk,* everyone jumped, including Sabrina.

Screaming for their lives, they rushed to the alien autopsy room. Bulbous-headed aliens lay peacefully on the operating tables as mad scientists in lab coats bent over them. Then came the flash of a meteorite, accompanied by an eerie whine, followed by strobe lights and fog. Whatever it was, it reanimated the alien corpses, and they lurched to life, chasing the shrieking scientists and onlookers deeper into the maze.

From here on out, it was pure Monster Mash. Freddy Krueger lunged at them from one of the kilns; ominous shapes lurched out of the fog; snarling monsters jumped from every nook and hiding place. No one needed to tell the ten-year-olds to run or to scream. They fled toward the exit, with their elders close behind them.

When Sabrina caught up with the frightened visitors, they were outside, having their pictures taken and being interviewed for TV. There was such Halloween spirit that the lady from the TV station was interviewing the lady from the newspaper.

"That was wonderful!" exclaimed Janice Raymond. "The Halloween Machine is going to be the high point of the season. I can't wait to go through it again!"

"Music to my ears," said a satisfied voice. Sabrina turned to see Mr. Kraft smiling amiably. He took out his calculator and began punching numbers into it. "And if we have thirty percent repeat business, there will be enough money to buy new curtains for the teacher's lounge!"

"See, I told you everything would be okay," Sabrina said smugly.

Mr. Kraft twitched slightly and bent down to whisper. "But what about the ghost? You don't think he'll come back, do you?"

"What ghost?" She looked at him as if she thought he was crazy.

Mr. Kraft twitched even more. "I could have sworn there was *something* here last night. But Zelda told me it was just indigestion from eating too much pizza."

"Aunt Zelda is never wrong," said Sabrina with a smile.

Mr. Kraft walked away, muttering to himself. Sabrina had just started back to the concession stand, when she heard a hissing sound coming from the doorway. She turned to see a gruesome ashen-faced zombie waving to her, so of course she rushed right over.

"How is it going?" whispered Harvey.

"Great! You guys really put a scare into them!" She bounced closer to him, then backed away. "I'd kiss you, but you're kind of putrid."

"What are you doing now?"

"I'm helping Valerie deal with the press."

"Can I give you a hand?" Harvey gripped one of his sallow hands and pulled it completely out of the sleeve of his frayed jacket. He offered the rubber hand to Sabrina with a ghoulish smile.

Sabrina grinned at her funny boyfriend. "Anytime."

"Salem, would you like more lobster?" cooed Aunt Zelda as she spooned another helping of people food into his dish.

"Don't mind if I do," answered the black cat, swishing his tail contentedly. "It's nice to be able to eat inside the house again."

"We were so wrong," said Hilda, as she adjusted Salem's lobster bib. "How could we have been so mean to you while letting that stupid hobgoblin take over the house? Mother always told us not to trust a hobby."

"That's what happens when the help gets too high and mighty," said Salem with disapproval. "I won't have to go to the pet psychologist again, will I?"

"No," answered Zelda. "Not unless you want to go."

"I'd rather see a Swedish masseuse," remarked the cat.

"Whatever you say," said Aunt Hilda, picking up the telephone. "I'll make an appointment for you."

"Ah," said the black cat, "it's good to have things back to normal."

About the Author

John Vornholt has done many things in his life, from being a factory worker to being a stuntman, but writing has always been his first love. He's written for magazines, television, movies, the theater, and computer companies, and he really enjoys writing books and telling a story one reader at a time.

John lives with his wife, two kids, and two dogs in Arizona. Check out his Web page at http://www.sff.net/people/vornholt.

DON'T MISS THE MAGIC! SUBSCRIBE TO SABRINA COMICS TODAY AND $AVE!! AND BE SURE TO WATCH MY HIT TV SHOW!

☐ **SABRINA THE TEENAGE WITCH** **$15.00**
TWELVE-ISSUE COMIC BOOK SUBSCRIPTION ($17.00-CANADA)
(PLUS YOU GET A THIRTEENTH ISSUE FREE!)

THAT'S A TOTAL SAVINGS OF $7.75!

☐ **SABRINA THE TEENAGE WITCH** **$7.50**
SIX-ISSUE COMIC BOOK SUBSCRIPTION ($8.50-CANADA)
(SUBSCRIBE & SAVE $3.00 OFF THE COVER PRICE!)

STILL AVAILABLE!

☐ **SABRINA THE TEENAGE WITCH ORIGINAL #1** **$2.50**
(COLLECTORS EDITION COMES POLY-BAGGED WITH BACKING BOARD) ($3.00-CANADA)

OFFER EXPIRES JUNE 30, 1999!
AVAILABLE IN U.S. & CANADA ONLY.
All Canadian orders payable in U.S. funds.
PLEASE ALLOW 6-8 WEEKS DELIVERY.

TOTAL AMOUNT ENCLOSED $_____

ARCHIE COMIC PUBLICATIONS, INC.

Sabrina's Subscription Offer
P.O. Box #573, Mamaroneck, NY 10543-0573

NAME_____ AGE_____ MALE ☐ / FEMALE ☐
(PLEASE PRINT)

ADDRESS_____

CITY_____ ZIP+4_____ - _____
STATE

DAYTIME PHONE #_____

☐ VISA   ☐ MASTERCARD

☐☐☐☐☐☐☐☐☐☐☐☐☐☐☐☐

SIGNATURE_____ EXP. DATE_____ MO. YR.

9081   TM & © 1998 Archie Comic Publications, Inc.

Boys. Clothes. Popularity. Whatever!

Based on the major motion picture from Paramount
A novel by H.B. Gilmour

Cher Negotiates New York
An American Betty in Paris
Achieving Personal Perfection
Cher's Guide to...Whatever

And Based on the Hit TV Series

Cher Goes Enviro-Mental
Baldwin From Another Planet
Too Hottie To Handle
Cher and Cher Alike
True Blue Hawaii
Romantically Correct
A Totally Cher Affair
Chronically Crushed
Babes in Boyland
Dude With a 'Tude
Cher's Frantically Romantic Assignment
Southern Fried Makeover
Bettypalooza

1202-12